Critical Cover-Up

by

Margie Miklas

Critical Cover-Up
Copyright © 2017 Margie Miklas
ISBN: 978-0-9986953-0-3
Library of Congress Number: 2017901870
Edited by Susan Hughes

All rights reserved. No part of this book may be reproduced, stored in a retrieval system, or transmitted in any form or by any means without the prior written permission of the publishers.

While influenced by actual events, this book is in its entirety a work of fiction. All characters' names have been invented, all characters have been created, and all incidents have been fictionalized.

La Maison Publishing, Inc.
Vero Beach, Florida
The Hibiscus City
www.lamaisonpublishing.com

Dedication

For all critical care nurses

Chapter 1

Just before sunset Wednesday evening, still in his blood-spattered green OR scrubs, Dr. Joe Connolly sauntered out to the parking garage, thrilled not to be on call tonight. The forty-year-old, six-foot-tall, muscular surgeon with his GQ good looks and personality to match smiled as he envisioned a romantic dinner and plenty of uninterrupted time with a certain ICU nurse. The perfect prescription for satiating himself physically and forgetting his ex-wife.

Before he had a chance to finish the daydream, reality struck him in the back of the head in the form of a .38 bullet; he died instantly, slumping to the ground ten feet from his black Porsche 911 as a tall thin figure slipped from the far end of the parking structure unnoticed.

***

Leaving the hospital at the end of an interminably long and arduous shift, Tracy Santini trudged toward her car at the back of the parking garage. Too tired to focus on her surroundings, she was suddenly frozen in her tracks by what she saw a few strides away. A man lay sprawled on the ground, completely still.

Initially stunned, her nursing instincts emerged and she approached the person. What she saw horrified her: the body was that of the medical director, Dr. Connolly!

Oh my God! Please don't let this be happening. Tracy shook him, shouting, "Dr. Connolly! Dr. Connolly! Can you hear me?"

No reaction, no movement. She listened for signs of breathing and checked his pulse. Finding neither, she fished out her cell phone, contacted the main desk, and directed the operator to call a Code Blue in her present location.

With years of nursing experience and advanced training in resuscitation protocols, Tracy jumped into action. From what she could gather, Connolly had been down awhile.

She worked hard to revive him—two long minutes that seemed like an eternity—until the code team arrived with a mobile crash cart. "Let me take over compressions," a male ER paramedic demanded. "How long have you been doing CPR?"

Tracy removed her hands as the paramedic took over. "About two minutes," she replied. "I called a Code Blue immediately upon finding him."

Two ER nurses, the physician, a paramedic, and two respiratory therapists surrounded the patient as they worked together to revive him. One of the RTs began to deliver timed artificial breaths and oxygen with an Ambu bag affixed tightly to Dr. Connolly's face.

The paramedic stopped the chest compressions and checked for a pulse. Unable to find one, he continued CPR. Next, the ER physician inserted a flexible tube into Dr. Connolly's trachea so he could be artificially ventilated, while a nurse attached the automatic external defibrillator pads. When the heart rhythm appeared on the screen, the code team viewed the flat line while the machine determined the rhythm and announced the next instruction.

"No shock. Continue CPR," announced the robot-like programmed voice from the AED.

Another RN started an IV in Connolly's right forearm and administered epinephrine while CPR continued.

After two more minutes of CPR, the ER physician said, "Check for a pulse."

"No pulse," and CPR continued.

If the members of the code team had any feelings regarding resuscitating one of their own, they didn't reveal them and, like well-trained robots, assiduously followed the protocols they knew so well. Observing from nearby, Tracy was grateful she'd been able to hand the code over to the team on duty.

The ER nurse resumed chest compressions, and the respiratory therapist ensured that Dr. Connolly received 100 percent oxygen. Just after the second dose of epinephrine was given, the respiratory therapist noticed the blood pooling beneath Dr. Connolly's head. He pointed it out to the ER physician, who turned the victim's head to one side and noticed the gunshot wound and much more blood.

"This is pointless. Stop everything," said the ER physician. "What's the time of death?"

"Nine forty-five."

Tracy had stayed at the scene in the event she'd be needed. And now, with the brutal realization that Dr. Connolly, a man she admired and liked—a man everyone respected—was dead, she wondered who could have done such a terrible thing.

As a seasoned ER staff, the code team had seen their share of blood and guts, but this casualty had shaken them, since Dr. Connolly was one of their own. As they packed up their equipment, they whispered among themselves, wiping away tears.

The nursing supervisor, who had arrived shortly after the code team began working, was on her cell phone the moment she realized Dr. Connolly had been a gunshot victim. She called the police and then questioned members of the hospital security team who'd gathered around, to determine if they'd seen any suspicious activity in or near the parking garage in the last hour. "Tracy, I want you to stay until the police arrive. Since you discovered the body, you'll have to give a statement."

"Yes, ma'am."

The police showed up within a few minutes, cordoned off the area with yellow crime scene tape, and began a preliminary investigation. Soon thereafter, the hospital administrators showed up—CEO Rob Chapman, Chief of Staff Dr. John Petry, and Director of Risk Management Katharine Jenkins. Tracy knew they'd be tied up for hours, with the cold-blooded murder of one of their physicians. She gave her statement and headed home.

***

On the other side of town, thirty-five-year-old Allison Jamison hummed as she lit two candles and set the dining room table in her recently purchased condo in the upscale Dr. Phillips neighborhood in Orlando. Tonight, was a special night—the first time she was preparing dinner for the man she had been dating for the past month. Life was wonderful, the sex was better than ever, and she anticipated a quiet, intimate evening together. She felt a twinge of nervousness though, since he had not shown up for their date, nor had he contacted her to explain that he would be late. Allison had been texting Joe Connolly for the past hour with no response, and now she worried that something might have happened to him.

She grabbed her cell phone and punched in the number to the OR. "Hi. Can you tell me if Dr. Connolly is still in surgery? This is Allison from Surgical Intensive."

"No, I think he left several hours ago, the OR nurse answered."

"Okay, thanks so much."

Allison's imagined concerns shifted to reality when her phone rang five minutes later, the number unfamiliar. "Is this Allison Jamison?"

"Yes, it is. Who's calling?"

"This is Detective Derning from the Orlando Police Department. I'm calling about Dr. Joe Connolly."

Barely able to speak the words, Allison asked, "Has something happened, Detective?"

"I'm sorry to tell you this, Miss, but there has been an accident involving Dr. Connolly. I'd like to talk with you. Can you come down to the station right away?"

Speechless, Allison fell onto the couch in shock, her cell phone still in her hand.

Chapter 2

Two officers from the Orlando Police Department and two staff members from the crime lab examined the scene in the hospital parking garage for several hours. Once their investigation was completed, they cleared the area and approved the body for transfer to the District Nine Medical Examiner's Office, where an autopsy would be performed. Detective Derning had already left the scene and was headed to the Orlando Police Department on Pershing Avenue to interview Allison Jamison. While at the crime scene he had noticed five recent text messages from her on the cell phone belonging to Dr. Connolly. There were two additional texts from the same number after the police had arrived on scene.

Derning, a seasoned, middle-aged detective with thinning grey hair, had investigated violent crimes for the Homicide Unit for the past five years. Prior to that, he had worked as a homicide detective in Brooklyn. After introducing himself, he unbuttoned his ill-fitting charcoal jacket and sat down at a table across from Allison. "I am sorry to be the one to tell you this, Miss Jamison, but Dr.

Connolly was found dead in the hospital parking garage. He was shot in the back of the head."

Visibly shaken and unable to speak, Allison sobbed, shaking her head. She was a petite, attractive young woman with jet-black hair that framed her face in a way that accentuated her captivating blue eyes. The detective estimated her to be in her early thirties, although she could easily have passed for someone younger. She pulled her knees up to her chest, tucked herself into a tight ball, and rocked in the chair. She kept shaking her head, as if to toss the painful news from her mind.

"I apologize, but I have to ask you some questions, and then I'll escort you home if you'd like. We'll make this brief."

Allison nodded, still not saying anything. She tried to gain some sense of composure, despite being in a state of shock. "I don't know how much help I will be," she said between sobs, "but I'll try to answer your questions."

"Okay. Thank you, Miss Jamison."

"Please, call me Allison."

She confirmed that she was an RN at Orlando Memorial and that she and Dr. Connolly had only been dating for the past month. "I had expected him for dinner tonight, and when I didn't hear anything, I started sending text messages but got no reply."

"Do you know if Dr. Connolly had any family, either here or elsewhere?"

"He was divorced. He didn't have any children, as far as I know."

"What about next of kin? Parents? Siblings?"

"I think his father lives up north somewhere, and his mother lives in Tampa. His parents divorced and the mother remarried. I don't know their names or any specifics of where they live though. I'm sorry."

"No problem. We can get that information. You've been very helpful. You two were pretty close I assume? You had a romantic relationship?"

"Yes, we did."

"Miss Jamison, Allison, did you know of any problems he was having? Financial issues, lawsuits, drugs? Any problems with his patients or at the hospital?"

"No, none. Everyone loved him. He was a great surgeon and was respected by all the nurses. I can't believe anyone would have wanted him dead."

"All right, Allison. I think we're done now. Can I escort you back to your home?"

"No. But thank you, Detective. I'm okay. I drive at night a lot, especially when I'm on call."

"Are you sure? It's no problem."

"Yes, I'm sure. Thank you. Good night." Allison drove herself home but saw nothing on the way, as if she was on autopilot. Once inside her condo, she lay down on her new couch and wept.

Chapter 3

Two months had gone by since Joe's death, and his murder remained unsolved. Allison had taken two weeks of personal leave, and although an emptiness still existed, she knew she needed to be productive. She was grateful to immerse herself in the hospital work that she loved.

The constant shrill ringing of the red alarm on the cardiac monitor almost made Allison jump out of her seat. As she rushed to Room 4 at the end of the unit, she heard the overhead announcement, "Code Blue Surgical Intensive." Her adrenaline spiked in anticipation of the crisis, and her heart pounded in her chest. *Thank God it's not my patient.* When she reached the room, she saw an elderly patient, his face a cyanotic shade of blue. He appeared unresponsive.

Dave Kellen, the competent and calm night shift charge nurse, began providing artificial respirations with additional oxygen, while two coworkers, Melanie and Karen, worked with efficiency to attach the defibrillator pads and place the backboard between the patient and the mattress to provide a firm surface for performing CPR. Glancing at the patient monitor, Allison could see that his heart rate had slowed to thirty-six, and the blood pressure cuff was not registering.

"He has no pulse. Start compressions. Allison, you're the recorder," Dave directed as the code leader. Once the code board was in place, Melanie began chest compressions. Allison picked up the code sheet which was hanging from the crash cart and immediately began to document the events.

Respiratory therapy and the ER physician arrived in less than a minute. While pushing an amp of atropine through the patient's IV line, Karen updated the ER doctor.

"He's a post-op thoracotomy patient from two days ago and had been stable on a Venti-mask. I heard the alarm, and when I came into his room, his mask was off, his face was blue, and he wasn't responding. I think he had a respiratory arrest and then *brady'd* down," she explained, referring to the slow heart rate.

As the respiratory therapist prepared to intubate the patient, the ER doctor asked, "Does he have a pulse?"

Stopping compressions for a few seconds, Melanie felt the patient's groin for a pulse. "I don't feel a pulse."

"Continue compressions and give an amp of epi." The crash cart was open, and Karen already had the epinephrine ready to inject, as she knew the protocols backward and forward. All the nurses in ICU had to maintain proficiency in Advanced Cardiac Life Support and had numerous opportunities to hone their skills and gain valuable hands-on experience in code situations like this. ACLS was one competency in which everyone made sure they knew what to do, since these were truly life and death situations.

To a bystander, the nonstop scene might have seemed chaotic, but everybody had a task to perform and things worked well. In addition to those already in the room, a lab tech showed up, as well as an EKG tech and a nursing supervisor. Within a minute or two after the start of the code, the patient had been intubated and another respiratory therapist was ready with the ventilator, so the patient could be mechanically ventilated for now.

Dave asked, "Did anyone contact the family?" A secretary indicated that she would get the family on the phone.

After the epinephrine had time to circulate and the patient was ventilated, his pulse returned and he had a blood pressure that was adequate. His color was no longer blue and his skin was warm and dry, so the Code Blue ended.

"Good job, everyone," Dave said. All involved felt good that a life had been saved.

"Are you ready for the x-ray?" asked the radiology tech, pushing his machine into the room to shoot the chest film which would verify proper placement of the endotracheal tube.

"Do you need anything else from me?" the ER doc inquired.

"Just your signature on the code sheet, please, and we'll need the order for Diprivan so we can maintain sedation while he's on the vent," said Dave.

Karen reached the family by phone, explained what had happened, and then contacted the patient's doctors to update them. The rest of the nurses left the room to attend to their own patient assignments.

Handing the code sheet to Dave, Allison said, "I know you need to double check everything here. Please let me know if I missed anything before you turn it in. Thanks, Dave." She smiled, invigorated, with a renewed sense of purpose. "We got him back pretty quickly."

"Yeah, that was good. He looked pretty bad. I wasn't sure if we were going to be able to resuscitate him," Melanie said.

I love being a nurse, Allison thought, still experiencing the adrenaline rush. Events like this contributed to a sense of camaraderie among the staff. Her occasional frustrations over the incessant documentation and hours of duplicate charting melted into the background.

Allison had participated in just a few codes before now, so she lacked confidence to assume the role as leader, but she liked the involvement and learning. She felt comfortable doing the transcribing, and in past codes she had performed cardiac compressions as well as ventilated the patient with the Ambu bag attached to oxygen. She had not run a code nor had she ever been the one giving the IV medications, so she knew that she needed more experience before she could feel at ease with these ICU emergencies.

After Allison's shift ended at 7:15 a.m., she drove home, still wired from the events of the night. In her mind she reviewed the code several times. Her OCD tendencies forced her into this ritual after any serious situation at work, and sometimes she couldn't stop obsessing about it. She had difficulty falling asleep some mornings because she was so hyper from everything that had happened on her shift. After a hot shower, she checked her email and flopped into her bed at nine o'clock. Exhausted, she fell asleep almost as soon as she closed her eyes.

***

Jolted awake by the ringing of her cell phone, Allison answered in a deep, groggy voice. The familiar enthusiastic

Critical Cover-Up

greeting of Jamie, her longtime real estate friend, brought Allison to life.

"Hey, girlfriend! Long time no see. What's going on?"

"Jamie, it's so good to hear your voice. What time is it? I'm just waking up, and it's been a busy week—last night, especially. One of the patients coded and I got to participate."

"Sounds exciting but also exhausting. I don't know how you nurses do it. It takes a lot of energy to save lives every day. I give you a lot of credit, Allison. Do you ever regret leaving the real estate office?"

"No. I love making a difference in my patients' lives. Closing a sale on a house can't compare to last night, no matter how much more money I might've earned."

"It's three o'clock. I hope you had enough sleep. Are you up for some karaoke tonight?"

Allison welcomed a chance to get out instead of staying in to study. She spent long hours on her days off reading critical care books, as well as journal articles from the American Association of Critical Care Nurses (AACN) website. She knew there was so much more to learn, so she tried to educate herself on the latest protocols from the American Heart Association and read medical news from Medscape. She realized the need to be a little more balanced, so Jamie's phone call came at a good time. "Okay, count me in. I do need some time away from all this seriousness. But no singing for me. I'll be ready by nine."

After a few days off and a night out with her good friend Allison was ready to get back to work. As she walked into the hospital, she smiled to herself and felt full of energy. *I wonder what new and exciting things lay in store for me tonight.* Looking at the assignment board, she was pleased that one of her patients was Mr. Wetherly, the gentleman who had coded a few nights ago. She wondered how he was progressing and asked Connie for an update. Disappointment soon superseded curiosity, as Allison learned the man's condition had deteriorated. He was still on a ventilator, and three additional consultants were now managing his care.

"He's battling pneumonia and is in septic shock. He's requiring high doses of Levophed." Allison knew it was one of the strongest intravenous drip medications for controlling blood pressure in such situations. "Despite the fact that he's receiving several antibiotics, his prognosis isn't good," Connie said. "He hasn't regained consciousness, even with no sedation. I discontinued the Diprivan for blood pressure reasons and due to his neurological status."

"Has the family been advised about the gravity of the situation?" Allison asked.

"Yes. They live up north and are on their way down. We told them he might not live through the night. They made it clear that they want us to do whatever we can to save him, so he's a full code."

"At eighty-four and in his condition? I know I would just want to die in peace and not be hooked up to all this stuff. I don't think families have any idea what these patients go through sometimes."

"Tell me about it. They aren't here to see what we have to put these poor patients through. And even with a living will, it's not too cut-and-dried. Maybe when they arrive and see for themselves how it really is, they'll reevaluate their decision."

"I hope so."

Allison's other patient was a stable post-op gastrectomy who was still on the ventilator. *We've been getting a lot of these stomach removals lately. I wonder if it was due to cancer.* She knew she would be busy but could handle the case, which was a typical ICU assignment. She went to look for the other nurse who would give her report, grateful that it was a traveling nurse and not Connie Gaston, who was almost never ready. She was able to take a quick report and could start her assessments in a timely manner.

The unit was full, so it looked like her shift would be busy. They were also one nurse short, since someone had called in sick and not been replaced. Word from top management was the usual explanation: "There aren't any nurses available." One nurse now had three patients, and the charge nurse had one patient and an empty admission bed. This was becoming the status quo lately, and Allison did not recall the staffing being so tight when she worked her clinical during nursing school. Good thing she enjoyed the work so much that she didn't mind being busy. It was the frickin' paperwork she detested.

***

By 2:00 a.m. Allison had gotten caught up with her work. *Thank God Mr. Wetherly is somewhat stable.* Allison doubted that anyone outside the medical field would describe a critically ill patient in those words. It seemed like an oxymoron. His blood pressure and heart rate were maintaining within the parameters ordered by the physician, although he required high doses of vasoactive medications to achieve those numbers. As Allison reviewed the electronic chart and checked his orders, she became curious as to the events which led to his respiratory arrest a couple of nights before.

Unable to find any new information from the physicians' progress notes, she approached the central station monitors. *I know there's a reason he coded, and maybe I can find something here,* she thought. Zeroing in on Mr. Wetherly's information, she backtracked to the day in question.

She located his patient data screen and studied his vital sign trends. Her inquisitiveness became an obsession for a few minutes as she zoomed in to the time of the code. She sensed she was on the verge of uncovering something.

"What is this? Oh no. Do I really want to see this?" she said. What had triggered the alarm was not only a heart rate of forty-five, but an oxygen saturation of fifty, which was quite low. After more investigating, Allison discovered that the oxygen saturation had been low for an hour before he coded. The last time it had been within normal limits was an hour and five minutes prior to the code, and at that time it was reading ninety-five percent. The number consistently decreased from there until it reached fifty. She knew this was not good. The alarms for O2 sats were always set for ninety-two or ninety-three, since anything below that was abnormal. *Why didn't someone check on this patient when the alarms went off?* she wondered as a heated flush spread up her chest and across her face.

Allison then checked the alarm review for the same time period and found close to 100 instances when the alarm had been triggered for low oxygen saturation.

Her stomach roiled, and she swallowed back the wave of nausea that followed. *Why didn't someone see this?* She printed out the alarm events and also the patient's vital signs from that terrible day and shoved the papers into her bag. Glancing around, she noticed that she was the only one at the desk and felt relieved that she was not being watched.

Maybe she would reevaluate the information later when she had more time. Her gut informed her that something wasn't right, and she knew this information was something she had to save.

The more she contemplated what she'd discovered, the more anxious Allison became. She knew that sometimes nurses just silenced the alarms when they were sitting at the desk and didn't really investigate the reason for them. Most of the time it was insignificant and an annoyance, such as an irregular heartbeat in a patient everyone already knew suffered from the problem. But this was serious, and Allison thought she recalled a nurse sitting near the monitors for most of the night before Mr. Wetherly coded. She remembered that the nurse was Paula, an experienced ICU nurse who had worked in that unit for at least three years. Now Allison recalled that Paula had been sitting near the monitors that night and silencing alarms while she was charting. *Had she silenced Mr. Wetherly's alarms? Possibly. Probably.* But Allison had not witnessed it. She could identify the nurse, but she couldn't say for sure that this nurse had turned off any alarms, since she wasn't specifically observing her behavior. *But someone had to have silenced those alarms.*

The sense of unease didn't dissipate, and Allison wasn't sure what she should do. *If I don't say anything, nobody will know and nothing will happen to my coworker.* Allison had this gut feeling that if the alarms had not been silenced, Mr. Wetherly would never have had low oxygen saturation for a long enough time to cause him to stop breathing.

***

For the next two days, her stomach was killing her as she couldn't stop thinking about Mr. Wetherly's situation. *Is it my responsibility to say something? Will it make any difference?*

When she came back to work that night, she found out that Mr. Wetherly had died during the previous shift. The nurses had coded him with the family present, but the sepsis was too advanced and he didn't survive. She tried to tell herself it was for the best, that he would never have been the same, but she knew better. Mr. Wetherly never should have arrested in the first place.

Chapter 4

Andy Marchman wasn't exactly a party animal. He hated crowds, lacked social skills, and fit the description of what most would consider a loner. Having been raised on a pig farm in central Florida, Andy did not experience normal teenage escapades like most boys. After graduating from high school, he chose computer science as his field of study and obtained his AA degree from a community college. He completed his bachelor's degree online to lessen contact with other students. Andy was basically an introvert.

Today, as he stared at the black digital clock in his austere office, he pondered the career choice that led to his position as Senior Engineer, Information Security at Orlando Memorial Medical Center. A sly smile appeared on his pale face as he mused. *I'm as happy here as anywhere. I earn a living doing what I'm good at, and I don't have to talk to too many people. Plus, I run the show. No one questions me, and I don't have to answer to anyone.*

His inflated sense of ego and arrogant attitude hid other character flaws. Andy seldom dated seriously; he had a reputation for short sexual flings with some of the hospital office staff. These meaningless relationships served to stroke his ego as well as satisfy his physical cravings. What he lacked in outward appearance and attractiveness, he apparently made up for between the sheets.

Andy awoke from his mental contemplation to concentrate on the computer screen in front of him. He focused his attention on activity from two screens in SICU, the critical care unit where his mother died. He blamed the unit and everyone associated with it for his mother's death. Every time he allowed himself to remember that miserable week, a rush of adrenaline shot through his body. "I'll fix all of you," he muttered, grinding his teeth. This obsession is what drove his daily existence.

A little over a year ago his mother died unnecessarily after a botched surgery. He couldn't bear hanging around in the hospital room with his siblings and stepfather as they watched her deteriorate day after day following what should have been a routine surgery. After an autopsy was performed and he learned that the surgeon, Dr. Joe Connolly, had left a sponge inside his mother, Andy vowed to get back at everyone involved. *I hate that unit and I hate that fucking Connolly. They're going to pay.*

And these SICU bitches who think they're God's gift to the earth have another thing coming too, he mused. *Who do they think they are, trying to tell us that there was nothing else that could be done? Who died and made them the queens of this earth?* His loathing for the SICU staff challenged him to find ways to make their lives as miserable as his. And he had the power of the computer. *Thank you, God, for gifting me with these skills.*

Chapter 5

Bobbi Herschfelt had just poured herself a glass of Pinot Grigio after showering. She stared at the glass, her mind blank. It was nine in the evening, and she was exhausted after a fourteen-hour day at work. Today was Monday, and the week had not started out so well. As director over two critical care units and a stepdown unit, her days were full of stress from the time she arrived at the hospital until she went to sleep at night. She never stopped thinking about work, because it was her life. Her husband had left her two years ago, unable to deal with her incessant obsession with her job—to the point of ruining their relationship.

Although Bobbi tried to tell herself that he just didn't understand what it was like to have so much responsibility, deep down she knew that she was the main cause of the deterioration of the relationship. It wasn't the only time her work had interfered with her personal life either. She'd never been in love with Ray in the first place, but she'd married him on the rebound after a failed lesbian affair she'd had with Paula, another young nurse. Bobbi and Paula met when they both worked as travel nurses in a hospital in Miami, and they spent about a year together in a steamy, mostly secret affair. Eventually it ended and Bobbi moved to the Orlando area to put the whole thing behind her. She had never been comfortable with her sexuality and still had not reconciled herself to the fact that she was gay.

Even though the gay lifestyle was much more accepted than it once was, and especially in Florida, where hospitals seemed to be a magnet for gay nurses, Bobbi couldn't accept it in herself, having been raised with strict Catholic teachings. Even at forty years old she loathed herself because of this inner turmoil that she couldn't share with anyone. She had no friends and used alcohol to self-medicate when depression struck. She stayed busy all the time and used denial for everything else. It was quite convenient.

She ran her critical care units with an authoritarian management style, and everyone working there knew it was Bobbi's way or the highway. Under the guise of doing the right thing, she implemented many policies which were over the top and unnecessary in the minds of her staff. Bobbi knew it but didn't care. Her goal was to reign supreme in her units and maintain control over everything. Her micromanagement tendencies served her needs well, and she had the title and authority to do whatever she wanted at work. It was the one place she felt a sense of control.

Before Bobbi went to bed she checked her work email again. "Shit. What now?" she grumbled. Aggravated, she reread the message from Katharine Jenkins, director of risk management, asking for a meeting as soon as possible.

An issue had surfaced over an event that had occurred recently, and it concerned a report that had been sent to Risk from Corporate Information Security. "During the normal course of an internal audit, unusual computer activity in SICU triggered an alert. Apparently, there were two users involved at different times and days and on different computers. Both were from nurses in your unit, Allison Jamison and Paula Fisher. The unusual activity consisted of numerous queries of a patient's records after his death."

Bobbi's eyes widened and she drew a deep breath as she read Paula Fischer's name. The email went on to identify the patient as Peter Wetherly. Bobbi remembered his name and that he had died but no other specifics. The patient had died in SICU, which was not that unusual in a critical care unit, but the email explained that there were complicating circumstances with this particular situation. While he was in SICU, he developed a respiratory arrest which resulted in a Code Blue, and he was successfully resuscitated. However, several days later he died after becoming septic. Again, this was not that unusual a circumstance, considering his morbidity factors, which had increased after the code.

Bobbi was more than curious. According to the information from Katharine, the audit indicated each time the record had been accessed, as well as the specific pages and screens that were viewed.

Aside from being upset over the fact that there would be an investigation into this activity in one of her units, Bobbi was unusually paranoid. Nobody knew she and Paula had a history, and that was exactly how Bobbi intended to keep things. Paula worked the night shift, so it was not hard to steer clear of each other. If anyone in upper management or corporate found out about it, Bobbi's job would be in jeopardy. Even having Paula working in one of her units in a subordinate position was an ethics violation, but Bobbi couldn't fire her or force her to transfer, because

Paula could threaten to expose their relationship and Bobbi's closeted sexual orientation.

Bobbi was eager to talk to Katharine but knew she'd have to wait till the following day. She fired off a reply email, telling her they could meet first thing in the morning. She also sent an email to her staff, reminding them of the seriousness of reviewing electronic records that were not from patients assigned to them. Then she finished her wine and went to bed. She needed at least six hours of sleep each night, so if she wanted to go into work early to prepare for the meeting, she needed to hit the sack now.

Bobbi didn't sleep well, despite the wine. At four-thirty she climbed out of bed to get herself psyched up for the day. She arrived at the hospital at 5:20 a.m. and whizzed through her units, surprising the night staff. She was not in a good mood and voiced several criticisms to the charge nurses regarding the appearance of the unit, complaining about equipment that was in the hall and other trivial things. The charge nurses were used to it and accepted it, since they really had no other option. She was the boss and wielded a lot of power.

The risk manager was already waiting for Bobbi in her office and got right to the point, in her usual abrupt style.

"Do you recall this patient?" she asked Bobbi, who acknowledged that she did, but not the particular details of his hospitalization. Katharine briefed her on the salient points, zeroing in on the unusual activity regarding his electronic record after his death. Katharine explained that this was going to prompt the necessity for a Root Cause Analysis, and both of the nurses involved needed to attend, as well as the nurses who were the patient's primary caregivers the day he coded and the day he died. Someone from the IT department would be there as well, along with

Bobbi and Katharine. She scheduled the meeting for Thursday, October 8, and told Bobbi to make sure her nurses were in attendance. She would take care of notifying the others.

The purpose of a Root Cause Analysis is to determine differing factors in a process and how they affect the outcome. The goal is to identify the root of a problem and discover the how, when, where, and why, and ultimately establish a way to reduce the risk of this event reoccurring in the future. Through this process, which usually takes several hours, all the possible causes of an unexpected event are weighed and recommendations are made to change the process. The focus is more on the process than the individuals involved, but if it is determined that individuals made errors, an action plan, which may include negative consequences for the individuals, is adopted.

Bobbi left the meeting and texted her assistant to review the assignment sheets for the days in question and let her know who had been assigned to Mr. Wetherly on those days. She notified Paula and Allison first, before forwarding the same email to the other nurses whose attendance was required at the meeting.

A few hours later, she decided to call Paula to guarantee that she got the information, since she hadn't been scheduled to work Tuesday. When Paula answered the call, Bobbi was momentarily startled, never expecting her to actually answer the phone.

Chapter 6

Without any hard evidence, Allison didn't know what her options were. If she reported what she knew, what good would it do now? After all, Mr. Wetherly was dead. Who would really care, and what would they do? Her stomach was in one giant knot, and she wished she had brought her Prilosec with her.

After she took report, she worked quietly to get through her shift, glad for once to have a patient who was in isolation so she could just be by herself. She didn't feel like talking to anyone. Luckily her patient was lethargic, so she didn't have to converse much with him either. Allison was so caught up in this dilemma about the Wetherly case that she couldn't concentrate on anything else.

I can't talk to my coworkers, because I'm not even sure what I think. Working in isolation gave her a reprieve from the chaos of the rest of the unit and some time to sort out her thoughts, although they were far from clear, even after a twelve-hour shift. When she left the hospital in the morning, she felt glad that she didn't have to return until Monday and looked forward to a three-day weekend. Surely after some rest she could put this all behind her.

Critical Cover-Up

After what seemed like a short weekend, Allison came back to work refreshed. She had taken time to drive the hour and a half to Cocoa Beach, taking the long way to avoid the dreaded Beeline Expressway where she'd almost died in a collision years ago. The memory still haunted her sometimes. It was that experience and the months of physical rehabilitation afterward that motivated her to change careers and become a nurse.

She loved being on the beach, where she could walk freely in the sand and feel the wind blowing against her face. It was easy to forget about everything stressful in this little piece of paradise.

But once Allison was back at the hospital and opened her locker, the stress returned, and the memory of the weekend beach time was swept away. A small white piece of notebook paper fell out of the locker, and when she read it, her stomach tightened and a sudden cold sweat dampened her scrubs. The note, handwritten in black ink, was brief but to the point. "We're watching you. Don't do anything stupid." That was it.

Stunned, she froze and stared at the note. Paranoia took hold almost immediately. *Who wrote this? And what did they know? How could anyone know that she had been considering reporting what she thought regarding Mr. Wetherly? What else could this be about?*

She hadn't said a word to anyone at work, afraid that no one would take it seriously, and then they'd blame her for creating trouble. *Could someone have seen me reviewing the alarms? Or worse yet, printing copies of the alarm reports and vital signs records? Maybe the computer recorded my every move, and I'll be identified as the one who had reviewed the documents. But who would have written the note?*

It was time to go into the unit and get to work. A few of her coworkers had entered the nurses' lounge, as the night shift was ready to start. She shoved the note into her purse, closed the locker, and tried to camouflage any signs of fear by smiling and making small talk with the other nurses. It seemed ironic that these same coworkers were the ones who once helped make her feel comfortable as she learned the ropes in critical care, and now she didn't trust any of them. She felt alone but had to keep up the charade, at least until she could figure out what to do.

After shift report, she started her work and managed to refocus on her patients—the part of her job that provided the most satisfaction. She had been assigned a patient who had just arrived from the recovery room after an ileo-femoral bypass graft to restore blood flow to his legs. Her second patient hadn't arrived yet, but he was also in recovery and would be arriving soon, this one after a lumbar laminectomy. She loved surgical patients, so she was happy with her assignment.

Allison assessed her patient and sat down at the desk to complete the necessary documentation. As she entered information into the computer, she overheard two other nurses talking about a threatening email they'd received from Bobbi. She clicked over to her email inbox and scrolled through until she found what she was looking for.

"It is hospital policy and an ethics violation, as well as a HIPPA violation, to obtain any electronic information on anyone other than your own patients. Anyone who does not adhere to this policy will be subject to discipline and possible suspension. This is a serious matter." She closed the email.

HIPAA was the federal act that had been in effect since 1996 to protect the privacy of patients. Allison turned around and joined in the conversation with Karen and Melanie, the two nurses who were talking about Bobbi's email. The general consensus was that nobody could figure out why Bobbi had sent this email now, unless something had occurred involving an employee looking into patients' records without authorization. Karen and Melanie indicated they had no direct information or guesses as to a circumstance that might have triggered this.

"It must have happened in another unit," Melanie said.

Allison stayed silent at first, fearful of voicing an opinion. *This email must be meant for me*, she thought. *Apparently Bobbi knows I reviewed Mr. Wetherly's records after he died.* "Do you think this could relate to a nurse checking on things after taking care of a patient?"

Melanie and Karen looked at each other. "Why are you so concerned?" Karen asked.

Allison replied, "I don't know. It just seems odd that all of a sudden we would get this kind of email."

"Don't worry about it," Melanie said. "Bobbi probably was just in a bad mood or upset about something else. Thank God we work at night and don't have to deal with her and her bipolar personality all the time."

Allison didn't say anything else but was more worried than ever now. She was fairly confident that Karen and Melanie hadn't reported her for anything. The more she thought about it, she figured that someone in the IT department had been able to see that she'd gone into the system and reviewed those records. But Mr. Wetherly wasn't her patient the day he coded, the day she checked all the alarm events. Maybe it triggered some kind of internal alert, which was then reported to the director of the department. That would go a long way toward explaining

Bobbi's email, but it still didn't account for the note left in her locker.

Being somewhat computer savvy, Allison had heard about keystroke logging and wouldn't have been surprised to learn that the hospital's IT department had someone doing that full time. She had heard horror stories about people being observed covertly and later fired. *Okay, enough of this paranoia.* It was time to get back to work. Her next patient would be arriving soon. Allison had to put those other concerns on the back burner for now and get back to being a nurse.

She actually enjoyed the rest of her shift, as she admitted her post-op patient and had time to do everything she needed to do. The charting for a post-op wasn't as bad as it was for an admission from the ER, and for that she was grateful. The night flew by. Staying busy helped her forget the worries that plagued her earlier in the shift. By the time Allison left, she was ready to get some much-needed sleep.

She walked out to the parking garage with four of her coworkers but didn't join in their mindless end-of-shift chitchat. As she approached her shiny, white BMW M3 convertible, she immediately noticed that it had been keyed all the way down the driver's side. She was infuriated since she took great pride in the expensive vehicle and always kept it waxed and looking good. Allison knew without a doubt that this was not just some random act of vandalism. For an instant, she wondered if she should report it to the security guards but let that thought go almost as quickly as she considered it. It was highly unlikely that anyone had seen anything, and if they had, the perpetrator would have been long gone. She got into her car and headed home, cursing under her breath the whole time. *Fuck this hospital. I'm working my ass off and where does it get me?*

Angry that part of her next paycheck would have to be spent to pay the deductible on her car insurance, she began to calculate what the repair might cost. She tried to decide whether or not it would be worth it to file a claim against her insurance, considering the $500 deductible. If she claimed it, her rates might go up. She definitely didn't need this, along with all her other worries right now.

As soon as she arrived home, she made a beeline to the bathroom. Emotionally and physically spent, Allison stripped off her scrubs and stepped into the shower. The hot water soothed her tense body, and she let it flow endlessly, with no regard to the bill. The effects of the gentle stream worked wonders, and Allison had no trouble falling asleep as soon as her head hit the pillow.

By two o'clock Allison was awake, and she threw on some clothes before savoring a cup of coffee. She still felt tired and knew the caffeine would perk her up. Working nights was something she had gotten used to quite a while ago, and although she liked it, she always felt tired on the days she worked. It was one of the hazards of the job and one of the reasons many nurses could never adjust to a night shift schedule. This was also part of the reason that one of the perks of working nights was a considerable increase in pay, amounting to an extra $5 an hour. This typically added up to an extra $10,000 a year, so once a nurse got used to that extra income it was hard to give it up. Many of them stayed on that shift years longer than originally anticipated.

She had to go back to work in four hours and was beginning to dread the thought of it. Trying to push away any negative thoughts, Allison began reminiscing about the days when she'd had a social life and actually fell in love. Young and naïve, she'd found her soul mate, and life was one continuous blissful day after another. Wrapped in her lover's arms, she'd fall asleep each night with a contented smile on her face. His tender embrace and the loving words he'd whispered in her ear made her feel like a woman. It was sexy and exciting. They were pleasant memories she never tired of reliving.

They'd married in their early twenties, ages ago. Sadly, things hadn't worked out so well, probably because they'd been so young and without careers, unequipped to handle the responsibilities of the world. Like so many other couples in love, their happiness was not destined to last forever.

It was an amicable divorce, and they went on to pursue their educations and live their lives. Every once in a while, she had some phone contact with Sean, who now lived in California, and she was glad they had remained friends. He had graduated with a degree in computer science, and she majored in marketing and sought a career in real estate. To her knowledge, he hadn't remarried either. Now she toyed with the idea of calling him just to hear an objective opinion about the situation at work and get some advice about the threatening note and car sabotage.

Settling down in her favorite chair, a comfortable old recliner she'd re-covered with a soft, light-tan tweed fabric, Allison made the call to Sean.

"Allison, it's great to hear from you. It's been a while. How have you been?"

From his words and the tone of his voice, Allison could sense an enthusiastic reaction. After the customary small talk, Allison told Sean about her fears, beginning with the sad story of Mr. Wetherly's demise. She included her suspicions about Paula, explaining that she had no real evidence and decided against reporting anything. Sean listened for a while before commenting. "I can tell you're distraught over this whole thing, Allison," he responded in a calm voice.

Once she told him about the threatening note left inside her locker and the damage to her car, Sean seemed much more concerned and started asking questions. "Has anyone said anything directly to you?"

"No, but I didn't know who else to turn to since I can't talk to anyone at work or trust anyone there."

"How would you like a house guest for a few days? I have some time off coming up. I could come out and spend a little time with you and maybe put your mind at ease."

Allison was grateful. Sean knew she struggled with anxiety. Plus, he was easy to talk to and would provide a source of comfort while she felt so isolated. "I'd love it. When can you come?"

"Maybe within the next two weeks or so. Let me check flights and see if I can get a deal on Southwest. I'll let you know as soon as I get it all arranged."

They said goodbye and Allison felt energized, knowing she had an ally.

Chapter 7

Paula Fisher liked working nights. She reminisced about her first week at Orlando Memorial three years ago. She was forty and, after having been a travel nurse for the past ten years, decided to settle down and take a full-time position. With her years of critical care experience, she was hired immediately.

Soon after Paula started in SICU, the director of critical care resigned. The position was posted by Human Resources for two weeks, with the intention of accepting applications from outside the hospital as well as within. Ten people applied for the job, and after the interview process was complete, Chief Nursing Officer Linda Steeling hired Bobbi Herschfelt to be the new director of the critical care units. Bobbi was an experienced, enthusiastic, critical care nurse with middle management experience, and she met the criteria better than any of the other applicants. It would be her first director position.

As Paula read the email regarding Bobbi's hiring, she was caught completely off guard, confused as to how she felt about the news. She had never planned to work in the same hospital as Bobbi again. She certainly had never expected to be working in the same unit and as Bobbi's subordinate.

After she and Bobbi parted ways, they had not kept in touch at all. The entire affair had been secretive, and though Bobbi had been paranoid about anyone else finding out about it, Paula didn't have those concerns. She was positive Bobbi had no clue that she was working as a staff nurse in one of the units she would be managing. This fact alone made Paula a little wary; she had no idea what Bobbi's reaction would be when she found out.

The other piece of the puzzle was the ethical concern. Paula could imagine all sorts of red flags being raised if the administration found out that a director was responsible for evaluating the performance of a former lover.

"I wish I could talk to her," Paula said as she finished scrolling through her emails. She knew that was impossible, and she assumed they would both deal with it nonchalantly whenever it came up.

When they finally ran into each at the hospital, Bobbi was professional and treated Paula as if she was meeting her for the first time. Paula got the message loud and clear and knew how to play the game. It was apparent that Bobbi intended to act as if no former relationship had existed, but Paula knew she was holding the cards. Bobbi could never fire her or in any way jeopardize Paula's job; if she did, Paula could easily let it slip to just one staff nurse that she and Bobbi had worked together previously or, worse yet, that they had slept together. Paula realized Bobbi knew this, and she actually relished the reverse control she felt over her boss.

Paula was not one to get too worked up over things. Although her ICU critical thinking skills were excellent, she took shortcuts when she could and didn't always worry about the rules. Some even considered her a slacker, and even though she had heard such comments, she didn't care what others thought of her; she knew her skills were top-notch.

Paula came to work each day knowing she could pretty much get away with anything and there would be no serious consequences. Not being the most diligent nurse to begin with, Paula slacked even more and liked getting away with it. Knowing she could punch in late or stay overtime to finish her notes without getting in trouble gave her an immense feeling of satisfaction, control, and job security.

When Paula got a phone call from Bobbi late Tuesday morning informing her that she was expected to attend a Root Cause Analysis, she was stunned. She had no idea what it could be about or how she was involved. A Root Cause Analysis was a serious event in any hospital, and although most administrations emphasized that it was not punitive, no healthcare professional involved in the process enjoyed it.

Paula worked in SICU with this inflated sense of immunity from repercussion. Sometimes her coworkers couldn't figure out why she got away with things when they got called into the office for much more trivial infractions. The general thought, as with many things in the hospital setting, was "it is what it is."

"What is this about?" Paula asked Bobbi. She mentioned a patient by the name of Wetherly, and Paula instantly remembered him and the night he'd coded. She recalled inadvertently turned off his oxygen saturation alarms. She knew deep down that she had screwed up. Since he'd survived, she hadn't worried, but her slacking had taken on a much more serious meaning when he'd died a few days later from sepsis.

Critical Cover-Up

"The meeting is set for Thursday, October 8, in the risk manager's office at 2 p.m. I expect you to be there," was all Bobbi said before she hung up the phone.

Now Paula was definitely nervous, suddenly noticing tiny beads of sweat dripping down the back of her neck, and she unbuttoned the top of her shirt. She tried to replay all the events, from the time the patient coded until she went into his record on the damn computer after he died. Of course it was impossible to look back through the record again now, because she knew any query would be caught by the IT Department. They would have likely picked up on it in the first place. She couldn't believe this was happening. The next two days would not be good ones.

***

Tuesday night, Allison checked her emails shortly before midnight when she had a few minutes' reprieve from her patients. She found twenty new emails, most of which were useless, like the daily menu listing and suggestions for preventing falls in the hospital. The emails from Bobbi had to be acknowledged, so she went through those with care. The subject of one in particular caught her eye: Mandatory Meeting - RCA. After checking her schedule, she was grateful she was not working Wednesday night, because she would still be expected to attend, despite the time. She had no idea what this meeting was about.

Allison didn't think she had done anything wrong but now was even more nervous than she had been with relation to the other issues. She wondered if any of her night shift coworkers were also required to attend and hoped she would hear something tonight during her shift.

The unit was busy, with several doctors making rounds and writing orders. She had a moderately difficult assignment, so she got right to work and never had a chance to talk with her coworkers about the email until two a.m. when things settled down a little. She punched out for lunch and then sat at the desk to eat her bowl of tomato soup and a Lean Cuisine she'd brought. Even though she was legally on a break for which she was not getting paid, she was working, watching the monitors and charting in the computer as she ate. No one on the night shift ever took a real break because there wasn't time, and there weren't enough nurses to cover if you did take it. Although this was a clear violation of the Fair Labor Standards Act, everyone just did it and kept quiet about it. It was one of those things that belonged in the category of not fighting City Hall. The administration knew it too but looked away and didn't care, always reminding the staff that they need to take their breaks and clock out for lunches. Allison doubted this sort of thing happened at places like IBM, and it certainly never happened in the business world of real estate.

"Did you receive the email about the Root Cause Analysis on Thursday?" Karen asked as she pulled up a chair next to Allison at the desk. When Allison acknowledged that she had, Karen started a conversation about the incident with Mr. Wetherly.

Now Allison felt much more nervous, realizing she might have to explain her suspicions regarding the oxygen saturation alarms during the Thursday meeting. She had never been to a Root Cause Analysis and didn't know what to expect, so she asked Karen about it.

"Well, I'll put it this way—I'd rather have a root canal. No pun intended. They are no fun, and even though you didn't do anything wrong, you feel as though they might find something anyway. It's stressful, and I'll be glad when it's over. I heard they think someone had been turning off the alarms."

This was all Allison needed to hear. She excused herself and headed to the nurses' lounge. Her stomach was cramping, and she had diarrhea. She knew it was stress-related. Not only was she worried about having to voice her suspicions, but she knew she might be in trouble for not having come forward earlier.

Once again the distrust surfaced, but curiosity caused her to wonder about the process. When Allison returned from the bathroom, Karen was still charting at the desk.

"So who else do you think will be there?" Allison asked her, doing her best to sound nonchalant.

"Probably you, me, Melanie, Dave, Paula, Bobbi, of course, that respiratory therapy chick who was working that night . . . what's her name? And Katharine Jenkins from risk management."

"No doctors?"

"I doubt it. They usually aren't involved unless the incident was specifically about one of them. So, I guess we'll have to deal with it."

"Yeah, I guess so. I'm glad I'm off the night before."

"Lucky you. I'll have to drag myself out of bed at one o'clock after working all night and then come back that night. Night shift sucks sometimes. Why can't they ever schedule meetings at night?"

With nothing more to say and her appetite gone, Allison clocked back in and headed for her patient's room. Staying busy was always a good coping mechanism when she was worried about something. After her accident, she needed to take Xanax for a period of time as she developed anxiety that she just couldn't shake. She had a tendency to be nervous, but she usually managed without taking medications. She was hoping she wasn't going to have to start again now. Her mother had been addicted to tranquilizers and slept most of her life away before she died from a heart attack when Allison was a teenager. Allison had no plans to emulate her mother's life.

On her way out of the hospital the following morning, she checked her messages and found a text from Sean. He confirmed his arrival flight for later that day. Allison was elated; the timing could not have been more perfect. She texted him back to let him know she'd pick him up at the Orlando airport. Allison drove home, took a shower, and fell asleep feeling relieved, at least for a while.

Chapter 8

Detective Derning was getting nowhere in his investigation of Joe Connolly's murder. There were no eyewitnesses, and the damn cameras in the hospital parking garage were not helpful.

"I apologize for this, but with Obamacare and decreased reimbursement from Medicare, we have had to cut a lot of corners, and security is one of them," CEO Rob Chapman had explained during a recent phone call. "Even though we installed an additional hundred eyes in the sky, only about twenty percent of those cameras are live. Unfortunately, the one in that area of the parking structure was not."

None of the hospital staff they'd interviewed had a bad thing to say about Connolly, and even his ex-wife harbored no animosity toward him. His surgery mortality and morbidity stats were average, with nothing standing out in particular. He didn't seem to live beyond his means, and there was no evidence to suggest involvement with drugs or any other criminal element. *But someone wanted him dead. The question was who . . . and why?*

Derning was sitting at his work station in the precinct, his feet propped up on the worn desk. His mind was in overdrive as he tried to recall anything he might have missed in the investigation. When his cell phone rang and Allison Jamison's name appeared as the caller, Derning was surprised and felt a slight sense of excitement.

"Detective Derning here. Good afternoon."

"Good afternoon, Detective. I hope it's okay to call you."

"Yes, of course. How are you doing?"

"Not that good," Allison said. "Have you made any progress on the case?"

"We're working every lead, but to be honest, we're back at square one."

"I wanted to talk with you because I remembered something, but I don't know if it's important," Allison said.

"Every piece of information is important, Miss Jamison. I'm glad you called. Is this something we can discuss over the phone, or would you like to meet me somewhere?"

"I can talk by phone. Like I said, I don't even know if it's significant."

"Okay, tell me what you know. I'm taking notes."

"Well, I recall Joe telling me about a case he had over a year ago. It was an elderly woman he operated on, and she was in SICU for about a week. There were complications, and she died. Every time Joe lost a patient it bothered him, but this was especially hard for him, because the family blamed him. They never sued, but they were angry and demanded an autopsy. On autopsy, it was discovered that a surgical sponge had been inadvertently left inside the patient. The report didn't state whether that had contributed to the cause of death."

"Do you know the name of this patient, Miss Jamison?"

"Please call me Allison. No, just that she was elderly and that it happened a little over a year ago," she said. "I couldn't remember all the facts, and I asked another nurse from SICU if she recalled the incident. She'll probably be more helpful to you."

"What's the name of your friend in SICU?"

"Tracy Santini. She's a charge nurse on the day shift. She knows I was going to contact you with this information."

"Thank you very much for this. It could prove to be helpful. Would you have a phone number for Miss Santini?"

Allison shared Tracy's cell number and wished Derning luck in the investigation. "Please keep me posted if you turn up anything, will you?"

"Of course, Allison. Thank you again. Feel free to contact me anytime."

Once Derning pushed END on his phone, he spent a few minutes assimilating this latest bit of information. He knew he would contact Tracy Santini soon, but first he had some research to do.

***

Allison was sitting inside at a table for two when Tracy arrived at Bella Napoli. The hostess guided Tracy to Allison's table, and the two nurses exchanged a friendly hug before Tracy sat down. The enthusiastic young waitress took their drink orders and scurried off.

"Tracy, I appreciate that you had time to meet up," said Allison. "I'm a mess and I really had no one else to talk to."

"I'm glad you confided in me yesterday. How have you been? I know it hasn't been easy for you."

"No, but I'm trying my best. It's better that I came back to work right away. If I can help them find who did this, I'll feel like I'm doing something for Joe. So, I'm glad you actually remembered that patient. Anything you can tell me may help."

"From what I can remember, that lady was really sick after the surgery. She never did well and only got worse. One of the sons was always angry. He was a real pain in the ass. The husband and rest of the family weren't like that, but that son was crazy. They even had to have security make him leave one night."

"Thanks, Tracy. Maybe it will help. I think I'd be a little better if I knew why someone did this to Joe. Not knowing makes me feel so vulnerable."

"I'm happy to help. All of us feel terrible about what happened, but I can't imagine what you must be feeling."

"You know, Tracy, a lot of weird things have gone on here. I've been feeling paranoid myself. Someone keyed my car recently. I haven't told anyone at the hospital about this, but someone left me a threatening note inside my locker."

"Really? What did it say?"

"I don't want to get into it right now, but it was enough to make me not trust anyone. For some reason, I feel like I can talk to you though. The only other person I trust is my ex, Sean. He's flying out here from California, because I called him and explained what's been going on. He's really a true friend."

"I didn't know you'd been married before."

"Yes, it was when I was very young and naïve. Live and learn. At least the divorce was friendly."

They chatted for an hour, enjoying their meal and catching up on all the latest hospital gossip. Before they parted ways, they made a pledge to stay in touch.

"You'll probably get a call from the detective," Allison said. "You don't mind, do you?"

"No, anything I can do to help," Tracy said.

"Okay, thanks. I'm glad we connected here. I'll call you soon," Allison said.

They hugged and went their separate ways. Allison felt slightly better than she had since all of this started.

***

Derning sat in front of a computer in the reading room of the hospital's medical records department. After speaking with Katharine Jenkins in the risk management department, he had the names of five of Dr. Connolly's patients who had died within the past eighteen months. There may have been more, but these were the ones reported as having died under questionable circumstances. Certain types of deaths had to be reported to the state, according to Florida statutes, and all of these would have first been reported to the risk manager.

Sentinel events like this were required to be reported to the Joint Commission as well. According to their standards, a sentinel event is a patient safety event, not primarily related to the natural course of the patient's illness or underlying condition, that results in any number of serious outcomes, such as death, suicide, discharging an infant to the wrong family, performing surgery on the wrong body part, transfusion reactions, leaving a foreign body in a patient after surgery, etc. These are serious mistakes that warrant investigation. Hospital administrators view these in a negative light.

***

Derning methodically reviewed the discharge reports of the five patients. All were elderly and four were women. But only one underwent an abdominal aneurysm repair surgery. Mrs. Helen Blanking, age seventy-eight, had surgery on August 10, 2014. According to the discharge summary written by Dr. Connolly after her death, she was admitted and diagnosed with an abdominal aneurysm and had surgery two days later. Her hospital length of stay was ten days, most of which was in SICU. She died on August 20, 2014. Derning could find no report in the electronic record about a second surgery to remove a foreign object, but on the surgical record, the sponge count was noted as incorrect. The x-ray taken in the OR showed no foreign object.

The cause of death was listed as cardiac arrest, secondary to sepsis, although the official autopsy report was not included in the medical record.

Derning recalled Allison mentioning that the family gave Connolly a hard time and blamed him for the death. He searched the record further for names of family members and jotted them down. Paul Blanking, the patient's husband, was listed as health-care surrogate. Two sons and a daughter were also listed, along with their phone numbers: Peter Marchman, Andrew Marchman, and Patricia Holding. Apparently this was a second marriage for Mrs. Blanking. Derning now had four people to question.

The detective continued to peruse the woman's electronic record, hoping to find more information on her family members. The health-care surrogate form listed the husband as the patient's proxy, the person who would make decisions for her if she were unable. He was the one who'd signed the consent for the autopsy to be performed.

"Thanks for all the help," Derning said to the medical records clerk as he traipsed out of the department, his mind focused on his next move. He needed to review the autopsy report again to see if there was anything more specific than what he already knew. And then it was on to Tracy Santini.

***

It was now half past eight in the morning, and Tracy's cell phone rang while she was making breakfast.

"Is this Tracy Santini?" a man's strong voice asked.

"Who's calling?"

"This is Detective Derning with the Orlando Police Department. I apologize for the early call, Miss Santini."

"It's okay, Detective. This is Tracy. What can I do for you?"

"Your friend Allison Jamison told me I could contact you. I hope she mentioned that to you."

"Yes, she told me you'd be calling."

"Do you have a few minutes for some questions? I can call at another time if this isn't convenient."

"This is as good a time as any, since I'm off today and have been up for several hours. What would you like to know?"

"I'd like to ask you about a situation involving a patient of Dr. Connolly's. She was a patient in SICU about a year ago. Her name was Helen Blanking. Do you remember the case?"

"Yes, I do."

"Okay, great. She had surgery and was in your unit for a while. Is that correct?"

"Yes, she had an abdominal aneurysm repair and developed post-op complications. She was pretty sick and eventually died," Tracy explained.

"I understand the family was a problem. Can you elaborate, please?"

"Yes. The reason I remember it so well is because the family was disruptive and created a lot of problems for the nurses."

"Please go on," the detective said.

"She had a husband and three children who were there quite a bit. The two sons were the biggest problem, one more than the other. And he was even a hospital employee. Neither of them were the proxy or health-care surrogate. The husband had that authority. But the sons were always questioning everything the nurses did and were manipulative with the staff. They took up tons of time. Eventually, none of the nurses wanted that assignment because of the sons."

"You said one was an employee? Do you know where he worked?"

Tracy took a sip of coffee. "He worked in the IT department."

"I understand security had to be called once?" the detective asked.

"Yes, more than once. They were loud and belligerent and refused to leave when visiting hours were over. We had to utilize security on several occasions."

"What happened after she died, as far as the sons were concerned?"

"They were angry and demanded to have an autopsy. Even though the lady was so sick and they had been told her prognosis was poor, they blamed her death on the doctor and the hospital, on all of us. We assumed they would sue, but I don't know if they ever did. No one was ever called in for questioning."

"Do you know which son caused the most problem?" the detective inquired.

"No, I can't really say. They were both difficult. One was more vocal, but I can't remember which one," Tracy said.

"Okay, thank you, Miss Santini. I appreciate your help. We'll be in touch if we need anything else. Have a nice day." As Derning ended the call, he knew what he had to do next.

Chapter 9

With all thoughts of the hospital out of her head, Allison made her way to Orlando International Airport to pick up Sean, who was arriving on the 4:20 p.m. flight from San Francisco. She pulled into the airport cell phone parking lot to wait for a text telling her he was on his way to the baggage area. She didn't have to wait long. She drove her BMW to the arrival area for Southwest Airlines passengers. She hadn't seen Sean since he flew out to visit her after her accident. She was grateful that they had remained friends all these years, even at a distance, but she secretly wished things had worked out between them.

The wide smile on Sean's face left no question as to his excitement in seeing Allison when she pulled up to the curb. Standing there in a light-blue polo shirt and khakis, Sean looked like he could be a model for *GQ* magazine. Allison was elated to see him. She got out of the car to greet him, and he opened his arms and hugged her for several seconds.

"Look at you," he said before he kissed her on the lips. Allison was aware of a slight warm twinge between her legs.

"I can't believe you're really here. You look wonderful."

"Yes, it's me in the flesh. And you've only gotten more lovely." After loading his single piece of luggage into the trunk, Sean slid into the passenger seat and Allison pulled out of the airport and onto Highway 436.

"I'm so happy you came, Sean. I knew I could count on you."

"I'm glad I could take the time off. It's slow at work right now, so the timing is perfect. I'm not sure how long I can stay though."

"Well, any amount of time will be fine with me." They laughed as they talked about trivial things, catching up on each other's lives on the twenty-minute drive to Allison's condo. Once they arrived and Sean got settled in, Allison returned from the kitchen with two Sam Adams beers and a bowl of sourdough pretzels. No matter how much time had elapsed since they'd been together, whenever they saw each other or talked on the phone it was as if it were yesterday.

"You remembered," said Sean, approving of Allison's choice in beer. They relaxed and Allison explained in more detail how things were going at the hospital and about the Root Cause Analysis scheduled for the following afternoon.

"I have no idea how it will go. I've never been to one, and I'm really nervous. They might ask me about checking the alarm history in the computer. I know you're not allowed to check on patients' information unless you're taking care of them, so I could be in real trouble."

Sean nodded and continued to listen. "I don't think I would be as worried if I hadn't received that threatening note and if someone hadn't keyed my car. It all happened around the same time."

"That's what made me know I had to come out here. Someone must know something or have it in for you for some reason."

"But I haven't made any enemies since I started working here—not that I know of anyway. I have no idea who would have done that."

"All you can do is get a good night's rest and go into that meeting and tell the truth. It can't be that bad, or they would have fired you. And you haven't done anything wrong."

"But who would have written that note?"

"I don't know, but I'm hoping we can find out. Can you access your work computer from home?"

"I can only see my schedule and continuing education stuff. The doctors can access their patients' information from home, but nurses don't have that kind of access."

"Hmm. Let me think about this for a while. I may be able to gain access. Why don't we go out for a bite to eat? You must be hungry by now. It's after seven."

"Sounds good. How about something like Chili's? I love their fajitas. I think they have a special going on. Twenty dollars for dinner for two."

"Can't beat that. Now I'm hungry too. Let's go."

Allison was happy to have a break from her worries about tomorrow, and she enjoyed the casual dinner with Sean at one of her favorite restaurants. When it was time to leave, she glanced at her cell phone and noticed a voice mail from Bobbi Herschfelt. She excused herself and went to the ladies' room to listen to it.

The message was short and business-like, typical of her director. "Allison, don't forget the RCA meeting tomorrow at 2 p.m." That was it. When she returned to the table, she shared the information with Sean.

"Well, let's just relax and not worry so much tonight," he said with a smile on his face.

"I agree. I'm not going to let work stuff ruin our time together. Let's go back to the apartment and enjoy the evening. Maybe watch a movie."

"That's just what I was thinking, like the old days." They looked at each other and smiled.

Chapter 10

Bobbi was already seated at the table when Paula walked into the risk manager's office for the RCA meeting on Thursday morning. Katharine Jenkins welcomed her, and the others at the table nodded. Dave Kellen, the night shift charge nurse, was there already, and so was Melanie, another night nurse. Within a few minutes, Allison and Karen showed up, along with the respiratory therapist who had been on duty during the incident. The last person to arrive was a guy from the IT department.

"Thank you all for coming and for rearranging your schedules for this important meeting. Your input is important. As usual, this is not punitive but is meant to improve our processes here at Orlando Memorial." It was the same administrative speak that had become so familiar to Paula by now.

"Let me introduce everyone here." Katharine droned on as she welcomed everyone to the meeting by name and department. "Bobbi, would you please summarize the events for everyone?"

Bobbi detailed the situation with Mr. Wetherly's code and subsequent death a few days later. Then Katharine asked each person who was there during the code to describe what took place from their particular viewpoint.

Next, Karen addressed Andy Marchman, the senior engineer in information security, and asked him what he knew in relation to any computer activity on the case. In a businesslike manner, Andy informed the group that two specific computers had an unusual amount of activity on the patient while he was in SICU before his death, and even more unusual was that all the activity was generated by two users.

"Andy, can you identify these users and tell us from which computers the activity came?"

"Yes, ma'am. The users were both nurses who work in SICU, and the computers were both at the desk, the ones closest to the cardiac monitors. These computers contain the patients' history—cardiac rate and rhythm, blood pressure, oxygen saturation, respirations, and other vital signs down to the minute."

"What activity was so unusual that it generated an alert for your department?"

"The most significant thing is that both users reviewed alarm events on the same day, a few days after the patient coded, but not the day he died. One of them even printed out the record of these alarms. There were over twenty instances of alarm events this particular user reviewed. The other user also reviewed many of the same alarm events but did not print out a history. Some of the activity also occurred after the patient died."

Paula squirmed in her chair and averted her eyes, hoping no one would notice her discomfort. She fiddled with her hair in an attempt to discreetly wipe the sweat from her brow. She knew they had her. *How am I going to explain this?* She wondered who else had been checking the records. *I'll know soon enough,* she mused.

"Andy, thank you. You were able to identify these two nurses by their individual computer IDs, correct?"

"Yes, that is true."

"You identified them as Allison Jamison and Paula Fisher?"

"Yes, ma'am," Andy said with no show of emotion.

Paula's heart raced and her stomach knotted when she heard their names announced. Allison must have seen her turn off the alarms and decided to investigate. *Damn it! What is that bitch going to say?*

Bobbi spoke up, stating that Paula and Allison were excellent nurses in the SICU and reminding everyone again that this was not meant to be a punitive event, but one to determine the cause and correct a process, to prevent it from occurring in the future.

"Allison, what can you tell us about this situation? Did you, in fact, review Mr. Wetherly's alarms and print out a history? If so, what prompted you to do this when you were not even taking care of him the day he coded?"

Paula watched intently as Allison, poised and calm, took her time to respond. "It's true that I didn't take care of him during the code, but I was there. I saw that his heart rate was low, and he was blue when I got to the room. I was curious what had caused this, so I went back to review his alarms later, when I had him as a patient. I found that his oxygen sat had been low, and that is what must have caused the heart rate to drop and for him to code."

"According to the information Andy has documented, you found numerous instances of alarms going off for low oxygen saturation, and you printed them all out," Katharine said. "Why would you do that?"

"I wanted to study them and see if there was a pattern. The oxygen sat had been low for almost an hour before he coded, and I wondered why no one had noticed it," Allison said.

Silence. The pause seemed to last forever for Paula, who waited for Allison to say that she had witnessed her turning off the alarms. Nothing was said. *Why didn't she say anything? I know she saw me sitting there.* Paula's thoughts were interrupted by Katharine's questioning.

"Paula, you were the other nurse who reviewed all these alarm events. Can you tell us your reasons for doing so?"

With tears in her eyes, she acknowledged that she had been at the desk and kept hitting the silence button without investigating the cause of the alarms.

"I'm sorry, but after so many alarms constantly going off, I think I became oblivious to them and just didn't pay attention. After he coded I felt guilty and wanted to see how many times the alarms were triggered. I was shocked that it had gone on for so long. I don't really think it was all me, though, because no way was I sitting there for an hour."

Paula was trying to admit her part in this but didn't want to shoulder the entire burden. She glanced at Bobbi, who was sitting in her chair with a bored look on her face.

Katharine thanked Paula for her honesty. "Nobody is saying you did anything to hurt the patient intentionally, but the purpose of this meeting is to discover the facts and find a better way to do things. It seems that now we have something concrete to go on. Alarm fatigue is actually an important issue today, and the Joint Commission issued an alert about this very thing not too long ago. Hospital workers can easily become desensitized to the frequent alarms, and it has actually been a contributing cause of patient in-hospital deaths." She asked the other nurses if any of them had experienced this, and all admitted that they had.

"Andy, can IT adjust the alarm monitors at the desk to ensure that they can only be turned off by going to the patient's room?"

"That would be biomed's area, but they can definitely do that," Andy said.

The tone in the room turned more serious, yet no one was suggesting that any repercussions would occur. Paula knew that an action plan would be drawn up and implemented, but she still felt vulnerable to some form of reprimand. She didn't know how much her past relationship with Bobbi would help her out in this instance, but she was sure she would find out soon enough.

Bobbi took the floor and told Katharine she would come up with an action plan, to be implemented immediately.

"Andy, make sure to contact the biomed department as soon as possible and have them make the appropriate changes in the alarm monitors. And Bobbi, be sure to include that as part of the action plan," Katharine said. "I look forward to seeing the completed action plan by no later than the first of the week, after which the appropriate changes will be made to the hospital policy on alarms."

Everyone was relieved when the meeting finally ended, two hours after it started. Paula had no idea why Allison decided not to throw her under the bus, but she was happy about it. Maybe this would create a new level of trust between them. *Better to trust a coworker than administration. We'll see how it plays out later*, Paula mused.

Chapter 11

Paula Fisher had a lousy night and was glad to be leaving work and going home. The unit was short-staffed again, and she had a heavy three-patient assignment. Two of her patients were on ventilators, and the assignment was bordering on unsafe; this had become the status quo.

When she approached her car, she found both back tires flat. "Shit," she muttered. *Something isn't right here. It's too much of a coincidence that both tires would be flat.* As she looked closer, she found a large gash in the sidewall of both tires. "Great! This is all I need." As she glanced around the parking garage, she saw no one. *Damn security guards. Where are they when you need them?*

Taking out her cell phone, she called AAA, hoping it wouldn't take them an hour to get someone there to help. She was already exhausted. "I need a tow," she said to the dispatcher, providing all the necessary information. "Forty-five minutes? I guess it will have to be okay."

Frustrated, she dialed the hospital operator and asked for security so she could report the incident. She knew it was an exercise in futility but went through the motions anyway. What was more concerning than having to wait for

AAA was the worrisome thought as to who did this and why. After the recent murder of Dr. Connolly in this same parking garage, she was feeling paranoid.

As she waited for the tow truck, other employees ambled toward their cars. Allison Jamison was one of them.

"Hi, Paula," Allison said as she approached the newer-model white Toyota Camry against which Paula was leaning. "How come you haven't left? Is something wrong?"

"Some asshole slashed both of my back tires. See?" She showed Allison the damage and continued to express her aggravation. "I called security to report it, but they're worthless. You'd think they would have activated the cameras after Dr. Connolly was killed here, but I doubt if that ever happened. They're more worried about stupid shit like nurses reviewing a patient's vital signs and reporting us instead of real crime that goes on right under their noses. This place has turned into a piece of shit. I'm so over it."

Taking a softer tone, Paula continued. "You know, Allison, I appreciated it when you didn't blame me at that Root Cause thing."

"I wasn't sure what to say, Paula. Let's hope we all learned something from the situation. But you're right. I've become disillusioned too, about healthcare in general and this hospital in particular. I became a nurse to make a difference, and it gets harder to do so every day. I haven't even been a nurse that long, and I'm beginning to rethink the whole thing. You know, I recently had damage done to my car as well. I came out of work one morning and the whole driver's side had been keyed, so I knew it was intentional. Plus, I received a threatening note."

"A note? What did it say?" Paula was now even more alarmed.

"It was left in my locker, and it said, 'We're watching you. Don't do anything stupid,'" Allison said.

"You're kidding me. When did this happen? Do you have any idea who it was?"

"I have no clue. It happened just after Mr. Wetherly died, and then a few days after that someone keyed my car. Seems like too much of a coincidence. And now this tire incident with you. Between the Root Cause Analysis and this, it seems like someone has it out for us. But why?"

"I don't know, but I'm getting paranoid, to say the least," Paula said.

"I haven't said anything until recently, because I didn't know who to trust. I even discussed everything that's been going on with my ex, and he's here now from California. He's suspicious and wants to do some investigating on his own."

The truck from Gary's Towing entered the parking garage and Paula flagged him down.

"Looks like you'll be okay. I'm going to go, but we'll continue this conversation," Allison said.

"Okay. Thanks for waiting with me and letting me know what happened to you. We'll have to stick together. I don't trust anyone else either. Thanks, Allison. See you soon."

***

When Allison got home from work, Sean was still asleep in the guest room, so she didn't wake him. Instead, she showered and went straight to bed. By the time she woke up in the afternoon, he was long gone. It probably had been a good idea that he'd rented a car so he could investigate while she was either working or sleeping. She smiled as she read the note he left on the kitchen counter.

"Hi Allison, I'm doing more investigating. I have some ideas I'd like to check out, following a few leads. I'll touch base before you go back to work tonight. Text me if you need anything. Love, Sean."

Just knowing he was close by made her feel more at ease. She had to remember to tell him about Paula's tire slashing incident. Happy to feel she had a confidant she could count on, Allison heart fluttered as she reread the last two words.

Chapter 12

On the drive home, Allison wondered if Sean would be there when she got back to her condo. The unit had been fairly busy during her shift, but her night was uneventful. Sean hadn't texted her, and she had been too busy to call or text him during her shift.

Once inside her door, she realized the condo was empty. She needed to talk to him, but at this point she was also desperate for sleep.

I'll send him a quick text, and we can have a longer conversation later, she thought. "Just got home. Exhausted. Going to sleep. Be safe. Xoxoxo

***

Sean couldn't stop thinking about the turn of events at Allison's hospital. He was convinced that her curiosity regarding Mr. Wetherly's records was directly tied to the threatening note and the damage done to her car. With years of experience as a computer geek, he suspected someone in the hospital IT department, although he didn't know why Allison's record-searching would be significant. But he intended to find out.

He was eager to follow a few of his hunches and see what he could learn. As a senior information security engineer, he was quite capable of hacking into the most sophisticated computer systems and felt comfortable doing so. Allison didn't need to know his plan.

After doing some research the night before while Allison was at work, Sean had an agenda for today. He dressed and left Allison's condo, careful not to disturb her. Fighting the morning traffic, he drove his rental car to the hospital and found a parking spot in the garage. Walking around, he noted the cameras on each level and wondered how many were active. The only security person was at the entrance to the garage, and Sean observed that he was about fifty years of age, but he didn't seem to have a gun. *Incredible that after a recent shooting here, the security is still so lax.*

He walked into the hospital and was forced to stop at the information desk to state his business. A thin, grey-haired woman wearing a light-pink smock and a Volunteer name badge asked him where he was going.

"To the cafeteria. I'm meeting someone here."

"Okay, have a nice day." The elderly woman smiled and pointed him in the right direction.

Geez, she didn't even ask me for any ID, Sean thought. He checked out the cafeteria and purchased a coffee. While he sipped it, he noticed that most of the people were employees, and there were a few lay people who were wearing visitor badges.

He strolled out of the lunchroom, mingling with the crowd as he turned left and wandered down the long hall. Stopping to read the directory, he noticed that the IT department was at the end of a different wing, so he sauntered in that direction. A small, nondescript sign on a windowless steel door marked the location of the IT department. A locked keypad prevented him from entering. The hall was empty, and Sean wandered to the end where he leaned against a wall and pretended to focus on his smartphone. This way he could remain unobtrusive yet observe all activity in the corridor. After fifteen minutes of inactivity he headed back to the parking garage, paid the three-dollar fee, and drove off the hospital grounds.

Before long, he spotted a Publix shopping center and pulled in. He chose a location far away from the store and parked his vehicle so he could use his computer without distraction or being noticed. After he shut off the car, he opened his laptop and got to work. Within a short time, Sean accessed the hospital database and zeroed in on the IT department. The department listed eight active employees, and four were working today. He was searching for someone with enough seniority to have access to all the security records, perhaps the department head. *Here we go. Andrew Marchman, employee since February 2, 2010. Position: Senior Engineer, Information Security.*

Sean scrolled to the date when Allison had reviewed and printed the vital signs of Mr. Wetherly. Then he checked to see if Andrew Marchman had worked on that date and discovered that he had. He'd also been at work on the day she found the threatening note in her locker, as well as the day her car was keyed. *Even though this guy worked during the day, he easily could have monitored Allison's computer activity remotely,* Sean thought as he clicked from screen to screen. He was sure this was the guy who had it in for Allison, but why?

Chapter 13

Andy Marchman lived and breathed computers, and his job was the perfect way for him to avoid personal interactions. He had tried to establish relationships in the past, but whether they were with friends or dating situations, he always fell short. So now he just didn't bother anymore, keeping his desires to himself.

He had become obsessed with making people pay for what he considered were the injustices he had been dealt in life. Ever since his mother died he'd been determined to expose the corrupt practices he witnessed at his place of employment, particularly in the patient care areas.

So when Andy noticed that someone offsite had been making inquiries into the hospital database in the last forty-eight hours, he immediately began monitoring the IP address and started investigating the physical address from which the activity was occurring. It did not take him long to discover that the IP address was registered to a laptop computer owned by a Sean McNally in California. Nothing made sense about a person who lived that far away snooping into the hospital computers. He couldn't spend all day on this but made a mental note to track the GPS of the computer in question. It wasn't until late in the afternoon that he was able to find time to identify its physical location. Concerned about a serious security breach, he decided to take immediate action and left the hospital a little earlier than normal to check it out.

Following the GPS coordinates identifying the location of the hacker, Andy drove his Ford F-150 to a nearby Publix shopping center, where he saw a white Toyota Camry parked in a far corner of the lot. In the driver's seat was a male with his head down. Content to observe for a while, Andy researched the individual but kept checking to make sure the Camry was still there. He identified a Sean McNally, age thirty-seven, divorced, from Mountainview, California, employed at Oracle Corporation. *Bingo.*

Energized by a sense of excitement and power, Andy knew this was his guy. *Why is he here, and what is he looking for?* He continued monitoring Sean's illegal computer activity and was even more alarmed when he found that he had been reviewing the staffing schedule of the hospital's IT department, including his own schedule over the past week.

Suddenly, the white Toyota shifted into gear and headed out of the parking lot, turning left onto a side street. With his heart racing, Andy didn't miss a beat and followed closely behind. The Toyota slowed down for a stop sign and then continued through the intersection. As soon as Andy's vehicle cleared the intersection, he increased his speed and rammed his truck into Sean's car, sending it careening down the empty street and into a cement utility pole. The F-150 drove past the mangled car and headed back toward the hospital.

***

Deep in thought as he drove, Sean looked up in time to see a truck's massive grill bearing down on him. There was no time to react. His head smashed into the steering wheel as the truck rammed him from behind. The massive concrete utility pole was the last thing he saw before everything went black.

Chapter 14

Allison woke up, still groggy, and checked the time on her iPhone. Two thirty in the afternoon. Six hours' sleep wasn't too bad.

Checking her text messages, she found one from Sean, sent a few hours after she'd gone to sleep. "Left early this morning before you got home. I'm finding some good info. I'll probably see you later tonight. xoxoxo."

She was happy to have some communication from him and texted back. "Just woke up and read this. OK. I'll be here. I'm off tonight."

She didn't hear back and figured he was probably involved with something and wasn't checking his messages. She knew she'd hear from him eventually and wasn't overly concerned. She checked her Facebook timeline and email account. An hour later, she showered and threw on some yoga pants and a T-shirt.

Still tired, she made herself a cup of coffee, warmed up a leftover blueberry scone, and settled down in her recliner with a Jodi Picoult novel she'd been reading over the past six weeks. Within a few minutes, her eyes closed and she drifted off to sleep.

At five thirty she woke up with her book on her lap and realized she hadn't gotten too far, as usual. She found a text from Sean. The message was short, almost cryptic: "ID'd the threat. MARCHMAN in IT."

Allison read it again. Her fears were confirmed. *That sleazeball Andy Marchman from IT! Now things are starting to make sense.* She remembered the story Tracy told her about Joe Connolly's patient, Mrs. Blanking, who died in SICU. Andy Marchman was one of her sons, and he'd been angry. *OMG, he was targeting me even though I had nothing to do with that patient.* She texted Sean a second time. "Just woke up from a nap to find this. Let me know when you can talk. I'm nervous."

Allison waited impatiently for Sean's reply. When it didn't come she decided to watch the local news to pass the time. She flipped on the Sony 42-inch TV and scrolled through the channels until she found the one she wanted. The female reporter's words caught her attention. "Orlando police are investigating another hit-and-run accident that occurred less than an hour ago south of downtown. Police responded to a call at 4:50 p.m. about a crashed vehicle on Sylvan Avenue. The victim, a white male, was taken to Orlando Memorial Medical Center in critical condition."

Allison found the news story chilling. Immediately she wondered if this could be Sean. *I know I'm just being paranoid, but after Joe's murder and the suspicious events Sean had apparently uncovered, I don't know what to think anymore.* A million questions reeled in her mind as she sat staring at the TV in disbelief.

The reporter continued with the story. "The crashed vehicle was a white Toyota Camry with rental car plates. If anyone witnessed this accident, police ask you to come forward. You can call the tip line at 800-423-TIPS. The investigation is ongoing. More details tonight at eleven. Carol Morales reporting."

Stunned, Allison bolted upright. Sean's rental car was a white Camry. Allison rewound the program and listened again, this time paying more attention to the video. She wanted to see if they showed more of the scene.

She checked her phone again. Sean still hadn't replied to her last text. She punched in his number, but the call went straight to voice mail. She didn't leave a message. Tormented, she called the hospital and asked to be connected to the ER.

"Hi, I know you're busy," she said when an ER nurse finally answered the phone. "This is Allison, one of the SICU nurses. I heard about a hit-and-run and wondered if you have him. A young white male."

"Yeah, he was the trauma who came in coding about a half hour ago. He didn't make it," the ER nurse said.

Shaking and unable to speak for several seconds, Allison forced herself to ask, "His name wasn't Sean McNally, was it?"

There was a pause before the ER nurse replied. "Allison, you know we aren't supposed to disclose that information, but yes, that was him, according to his driver's license. Do you know him? We're still trying to find next of kin."

Allison couldn't utter a word. "Allison, did you know him? Are you there?"

She choked back tears. "Yes, he was my ex. He lived in California and was visiting me. I don't know about next of kin. I can't believe this is happening."

"I'm so sorry. I wish we could have done more, but we don't know how long he'd been down, and he came in coding from the field. It's very sad, especially since he's so young."

Sobbing, Allison eked out a thank you and ended the call.

She stared at her phone, tears flowing down her face, as she tried to absorb what she just heard. Closing her eyes, and shaking her head back and forth, she began to moan. Suddenly, her phone alerted her to a voice message. It was from Sean! Allison's heart pounded as her excitement negated logic. She quickly tapped the voice mail icon and listened.

"Allison, things are worse than I thought. Marchman's been monitoring you and your coworkers for months. Let the detective know, because this guy could be connected to that surgeon's murder. I'll be back at your condo in a few hours. Be careful."

Allison was completely overwhelmed, as if everything around her was sucking the air out of her and pulling the ground from beneath her. Her throat seemed to close in on itself, and she caught herself gasping for air. Her heart racing, she recognized the symptoms of a panic attack, despite the fact that she hadn't experienced one for several years.

Allison went through what she knew to be effective steps to calm herself down. In just a few minutes she was breathing normally and feeling better. She went to the medicine cabinet and grabbed a Xanax for good measure.

Now that the panic attack was over, at least she was able to think more clearly. An imposing sense of fear existed, but she was also angry. Angry at Andy Marchman. Angry that Sean was dead. *Was the voice message she just heard delayed? Sean must have called earlier, and somehow the call went directly to voice mail.* This had happened before for no particular reason. It was frustrating and illogical, but there was no other explanation.

Strengthened by her seething anger, Allison kicked into aggressive mode. She didn't know the details but knew enough. Andy Marchman was her enemy, and she was going after him.

Chapter 15

All kinds of thoughts were reeling inside Allison's head as she tried to sort them and figure out a plan. *I can't just sit here. I have to see for myself that Sean is really dead. Then I can decide what to do. He came out here to help me, and he texted me information for a reason.* Grabbing her phone, she called the ER again. With incredible presence of mind, she spoke clearly and without emotion. "Hi, this is Allison Jamison. I just spoke to someone about Sean McNally. I need to talk to the charge nurse, please. It's urgent."

Allison was operating on adrenaline. She only had to wait about a minute before a voice responded on the other end. "Carrie Bentley, Charge Nurse. How may I help you?"

"This is Allison Jamison. I'm a nurse in SICU, but I'm at home now. I called a little while ago and was told my friend Sean McNally came in as a trauma and has died. I'd like to come in to identify him. He's my ex, and he has no family here. He lives in California."

"Sure, Allison, that would be fine. I'm so sorry we couldn't do more. He's still in one of the bays, so when you get here ask for me," Carrie said.

"Thank you. I should be there in about an hour."

Now that she had some semblance of a plan, Allison focused, put on her makeup, and changed clothes. In thirty minutes, she was out the door and on the way to the medical center.

She knew traffic would be heavy at this time of day and prayed there wouldn't be any accidents to slow her down. Knowing the quickest route by heart, Allison arrived and parked in the ER visitors' lot.

"Carrie Bentley told me to ask for her when I got here," she said to the clerk sitting behind a glass wall in the ER entrance.

"Okay. What is your name, and can I see some ID?"

Allison produced her hospital badge, which seemed to satisfy the clerk. "Wait here. I'll call Carrie."

"Thank you. I appreciate it," Allison said, grateful for no delays.

The ER waiting room was packed, and she was thankful that she wasn't there as a patient. After five minutes, the door to the ER opened and a short, somewhat heavy, middle-aged woman wearing green scrubs emerged. Her face devoid of emotion, she was all business, the picture of authority and efficiency. She introduced herself and asked Allison to follow her.

As if she had blinders on, Allison barely noticed the patients who occupied the stretchers against the wall and inside the cubicles with open curtains. She was functioning on autopilot, just going through the motions, almost numb. All she was focused on was following Carrie's lead. Suddenly, the charge nurse stopped at a closed curtain, turned to make eye contact with Allison, and said, "He's in here. I'll give you a few minutes alone."

"Thank you" was all Allison could utter. She paused and then opened the curtain and slowly walked toward the stretcher. Tears filled her eyes and the scene became a blur. With the palm of her left hand, she wiped her eyes enough to see what confronted her. Beneath the stark white hospital sheet lay a motionless body. Whatever tubes or equipment had previously been tethered to him were gone. She recognized Sean, his face swollen and bruised, his hair covered in blood. A heaviness in her chest overwhelmed her. Allison stared at him for a full minute before reaching out to touch his hand. The tears returned and Allison cried silently, her heart aching. He looked peaceful, yet she couldn't deny he had been the victim of a traumatic act. Cold and lifeless, he was gone forever.

After ten minutes went by, Allison composed herself. She looked around and noticed a belongings bag, a clear plastic bag the hospital used to store the patients' clothing and anything else they had in their pockets when they were admitted. She rummaged through the bag and found Sean's cell phone in the right front pocket of his jeans. She took it and checked the other pocket. His wallet was still in it. She put both items in her purse. A part of her wanted to linger, but she knew it was time to leave. Taking one last look, she blew him a kiss, pulled open the curtain, and walked out of the bay. Carrie was busy at the nurses' station, and Allison stopped to talk briefly with her.

"Thank you, Carrie. It's definitely Sean. What will happen now?"

"His body will stay in the morgue, but he'll likely have an autopsy. It's up to the coroner. Once we make contact with the family and they make arrangements for a funeral home, his body will be moved to that location. We're still working on making connections."

"Like I said, I really don't know anything about his family. He just came out here a few days ago, and it had been years since we'd seen each other," Allison said.

"Okay. Give us a call if you find out anything," Carrie said. "Are you okay to go home, or do you want us to call someone?"

"I'll be okay. Thanks just the same. Good night."

An aching loneliness enveloped Allison as she wandered out of the sterile ER. Not wishing to return to her empty condo, she walked to the south elevator, rode it up to the second floor, and got off in front of SICU. Using her employee badge, she swiped the security reader and the door swung open.

"Allison, what are you doing here? Did you come in to help us out? We're short, as usual," Karen said.

Drained and expressionless, Allison replied, "No, sorry. Is Paula working?"

"Yeah, she's down at the end of the unit," Karen said, pointing toward Paula's rooms. "She has three patients, so she's already pretty busy,"

Allison proceeded down the hall and found Paula in front of a computer checking her patient's electronic chart. Paula looked up and seemed surprised to see Allison standing there in street clothes.

"Hey, what's up? What are you doing here?"

"Sean was in an accident. He was the trauma you were supposed to get, but he didn't make it. I came in to make sure it was him," Allison said in a matter-of-fact tone. Her throat ached and she pursed her lips as she tried to maintain her composure, but her eyes filled with tears.

"Oh no, Allison. I can't believe it." Paula got up and put her arms around Allison. "I'm so sorry. Do you know what happened?"

"It was a hit-and-run. I only know what I saw on the news. The ER nurse told me they had no idea how long he was down. I found a message from him later on my phone. He said he found something out about that creepy Andy Marchman. It's like he was trying to warn me, and now I'll never know." She wiped back the tears and continued. "I don't know what to do or who to talk to. I came up here hoping you were working."

As Paula gave her another hug, an IV pump alarm went off in one of her rooms. "Of course. I'm glad you did. I have these three patients though, and I'm already behind, so I can't talk right now. I'm really sorry, Allison. I wish I had more time, but you know how it is."

"I know. I'll call you," Allison said.

"Okay. Call me when I get off in the morning, if you're awake."

Allison ambled down the hall and out of the unit. Staring straight ahead, she moved like a robot until she reached the parking structure and was inside her vehicle. The only thing on her mind was Sean's cell phone.

Chapter 16

Allison put her BMW in gear and mindlessly drove toward home. Her heart raced and she loosened the top buttons of her shirt to cool off. With her left hand on the steering wheel, she grabbed a hair scrunchie from the storage compartment next to her seat. At the first stoplight, she pulled her long black hair up off her neck and twisted it into a knot on top of her head. Tears moistened her eyes, and she had to wipe them away with her sleeve to see to drive.

Her thoughts were focused on Sean's message. She wanted to see what time Sean sent her that voice mail. She was formulating a plan, although things were still sketchy.

When she arrived home twenty minutes later, Allison parked the car and hurried toward her condo. Once inside, she headed straight for the kitchen. She grabbed a cold beer from the fridge and flopped down in the recliner to chill for a few minutes.

She woke up two hours later, her beer warm and her time wasted. She bolted out of the chair, went into the bathroom, and threw some water on her face to clear her head.

Allison tossed out the beer and took a bottle of water out of the fridge. She picked up her bag, sat down on the couch, and pulled out Sean's cell phone. When she attempted to turn it on, the familiar slide to unlock it didn't appear on the screen. *Of course not, idiot. Sean always locks his phone. What was I thinking?* Frustrated, she got her phone out to listen to his voice message again. *Maybe I just need to hear his voice.*

She played the message twice, fighting back tears at the sound of Sean's voice. "Get a grip, Allison," she muttered, swiping the tears from her face with the back of her hand. "Do something."

She laid the phone on the table. *Sean wanted me to tell Detective Derning what he'd discovered. That would be a good place to start.* Before she could make the call, her phone pinged with a new text notification.

"Can you come in and work? We are swamped."

She didn't recognize the number, but it was obviously from work. "Probably a nursing tech or some secretary assigned to call staff in an effort to get someone to come in," she muttered. "Don't they know my ex is still lying in the ER?" *Morons.*

Aggravated, she remembered how many times she'd gotten a call asking the same thing, when all they had to do was look at the prior night's assignment board to see that she had worked all night and would probably still be sleeping at noon. So typical of them, and she was short on patience right now.

Five minutes later she texted back. "Sorry, I can't come in. I'm exhausted."

She leaned back on the couch and closed her eyes. *I need to call Derning* was the last thought she had before sleep overtook her.

Chapter 17

Andy Marchman sat in his office, sipping his morning coffee as he checked the hospital computer system database. *No outside activity*, he thought with an evil smirk. He was pleased, validated. It didn't matter who'd been behind the security threat. The important thing was that the problem had been eradicated—once and for all.

Now he could concentrate on other matters, like the SICU nurses. Fortunately, his department basically ran itself without him, since he was smart enough to delegate all the work to his assistant director, Jim Waddell, an experienced and extremely capable engineer who had worked there for more than ten years. Focusing on the computers in SICU, he reviewed the last few shifts to see when Paula and Allison had worked. He also zeroed in on any computer activity by their director, Bobbi Herschfelt.

Almost disappointed not to find anything out of the ordinary, he changed his focus to creating a few choice fake emails. He smiled, barely able to contain his glee at his own resourcefulness, achieving a much higher degree of satisfaction from his ingenuity than he experienced from his computer technology career.

First up, Bobbi Herschfelt. That bitch was in charge of SICU, the place that killed my mother, and she didn't do anything about it. She walks around with her mightier-than-thou attitude, barking out orders. It's time she gets brought down a peg.

For several years, Andy had been privy to some little-known gossip and decided this was the perfect time to use it. Pulling up the hospital proprietary email program, he crafted an email to Bobbi and listed the sender as the hospital corporate headquarters ethics department.

On the subject line he typed, "Urgent – Ethics Issue – Sensitive."

When he finished the message, he read it again for good measure. "Bobbi Herschfelt, RN, Director of Critical Care. It has come to our attention that you have had or are currently having an inappropriate intimate relationship with one of the RNs in SICU, a department you manage. You must know that if this is true, it falls within the category of an ethics violation of the most serious nature and will be dealt with accordingly. An investigation has been launched, and we expect your full cooperation. You will be contacted soon by an official member of the ethics board."

He signed the message as Evelyn Beardsley, Ethics.

That should give her something to worry about, Andy thought, smirking.

Next, Paula Fischer. She thought she got away with her lazy-ass habit of turning off the computer alarms. Next time she'll think twice.

Andy addressed a new email to Paula, filling in the subject line the same as he had with Bobbi's email. *What works for one will work for two.* The message was basically the same, notifying Paula that an ethics investigation had been launched into her alleged affair with her immediate supervisor.

Next, he created a phony email from Bobbi to Paula. "Urgent! Mandatory meeting in my office tomorrow after your shift. If you value your job and current position in SICU, you will be there. Bobbi Herschfelt, Director."

And a final email to complete the job. Andy addressed the last email to Allison. In the subject line he typed, "Password inactivated." *This ought to screw up the start of her next shift.*

Grinning to himself he typed, "Once you have opened this email you will no longer have access to your sign-on. Please come to the IT department in person in order to reactivate your online access."

He quickly made the adjustments necessary to close Allison's access to the hospital computer system, knowing that seventy percent or more of an RN's work is dependent on computer access and electronic charting. Satisfied, Andy signed out of his computer and headed to the cafeteria for his midmorning ritual of a donut and second cup of coffee.

Chapter 18

Paula had barely made it through her shift the night before. She was exhausted and slept all day, so she hadn't spoken to Allison. Tonight, was just as bad, and it was nearly midnight before she had a chance to chart. *It's like a repeat of last night. Jesus.* These three-patient assignments were hell and definitely unsafe. There was no way you could get all your work done. You just had to prioritize and do what was necessary and skip the rest. Paula longed for the days when she could slack off and read a book at work.

When her patients were finally stable, she opened her computer to begin her assessments. *At least I've learned how to streamline this process, so it doesn't take me an hour and a half to do three assessments.*

She noticed the blinking light in the lower right-hand corner of her screen, alerting her that she had forty new emails. Out of habit she clicked on the email program to scan them before starting her charting. Most were junk, but two caught her attention. She opened the one from the ethics department first.

A wave of nausea passed over her. *Who could possibly know about my relationship with Bobbi?* she wondered.

Then she read the other urgent email, this one from Bobbi, and the room began to spin.

Having no time to focus on these emails, Paula snapped back into work mode and began the tedious process of charting, only to be interrupted by Dave, the charge nurse. "Paula, I know you're swamped. I'm sorry. But we're going to do a lateral transfer of Bed 9 up to Medical ICU, because there's a post-op patient on 4 South who's septic and needs a bed here. So finish up your charting so you can call report."

"What the fuck? I just started charting on these people. I can barely keep my head above water here. You mean I'm going to have to take that crashing patient after I transfer one of these?"

"Yes. I'm sorry, but that's how it is. I thought we were getting a break when Allison agreed to come in at eleven to help out. She just got here a while ago, but one of the travelers had to go home sick, so she's replacing him."

"Allison came in? Dave, this really sucks," Paula said. "I'm so sick and tired of this. Every night it gets worse and worse. And no one in administration cares. Why can't MICU take that patient instead of us having to play musical beds?"

"I know. I suggested that option to the supervisor, but the patient is surgical and really belongs here. I'm going to send Allison down here to help you get him packed up and ready to go."

Seething, Paula wished she had never become a nurse. The job had only become more labor-intensive and stressful. Sure, the money was good, much better than when she graduated eons ago, but it wasn't worth it anymore. She wished she was old enough to retire.

Resigned to the inevitable, she started documenting the assessment on her patient in Bed 9 so she could call report and he'd be ready to go. She pecked hard on the keyboard, spewing four-letter words under her breath as she typed.

***

Allison punched in at 10:55 p.m., retrieved her stethoscope from her locker, and headed down the hallway without running into a single soul. The hiss of ventilators and chorus of alarm bells confirmed that the unit was busy.

Dave appeared from one of the rooms. "Thank you for offering to come in, Allison. I know you've had a rough time, but we really need you. One of the travelers is sick and has to go home, so if you can take report from him it would be great. You'll take over his assignment. Beds 3 and 6. They're both vented."

"I felt guilty not coming last night, but I just couldn't do it. This is the best I can do. So I'm here and ready to work." Allison grabbed a sheet of paper and went off in the direction of Room 3. A short male nurse was in the room, charting on the computer. Allison didn't recognize him.

"Hi, I'm Allison. I came in to help out. I guess I'm getting your patients."

"Yeah, I'm almost done. I can give you report now. By the way, my name is Lou."

"Okay, Lou, whenever you're ready," Allison said as she surveyed the environment around the unconscious patient. Within a minute she had noted his vent settings and IV drip medications and rates. He had two chest tubes and was receiving tube feedings.

Lou gave Allison a summarized report, and then they moved to Room 6, where the patient looked almost identical to the one in Room 3. By 11:30 p.m., Lou said goodbye and Allison was left to assess her patients.

Ten minutes later, Dave appeared at the doorway. "I know you're just getting started," he said, "but can you go to the other side and give Paula a hand? She has a heavy assignment, three patients, and Bed 9 has to be transferred so she can get a crash-and-burn from one of the floors. If you can help get him packed up and ready to roll out the door, that would be great. Thanks." He disappeared without waiting for a response.

I see it's going to be that kind of night. Assuring herself that her patients' alarms were on, she made her way to the other side of the unit to find Paula.

Allison found Paula inside a patient room. "Hey, girlfriend. Sucky night, huh?"

"Don't even get me started. Two in a row. Last night I had the night from hell. I didn't even know you were here tonight. What's your assignment?"

"I have 3 and 6, two vents. Not too bad . . . yet. Dave told me to help you pack this guy up."

"Yeah, that would be great. I still have charting to do and have to call report. I'm so disgusted with this whole place."

"I know. Me too. We'll talk later. I have a lot to tell you," Allison said.

"Okay. Thanks, Allison," Paula said. In silence they worked to accomplish their tasks without further delay.

Ten minutes later, the patient was ready to be moved, and Allison headed to Room 3 to assess the patient there.

When she logged into the computer, an alert was flashing, announcing an urgent email. The hospital computer program was set up so that she couldn't access anything else until she checked the alert. *What a pain.*

Obviously a nurse didn't design this stupid archaic program.

The highlighted email triggering the alert, titled "Password inactivated," had been sent by IT department security. Confused, Allison clicked open the email, which stated that she'd lost access and needed to stop by IT in order to reactivate her account. She stared at the screen. It sounded like a hoax, but this was a secure server. She closed the email program and clicked onto the medical portal. A black screen appeared with a terse message: "Unavailable. Contact your IT department."

Great. Just what I need. I'm already behind. She dialed the troubleshooting number for the after-hours IT department and was placed on hold. A robot-like voice stated, "You have reached the 24-hour IT department. You are in line for a specialized technician. Your wait time is approximately seven minutes. Please do not hang up."

Jesus, this gets worse by the minute. Eventually a voice interrupted Allison's thoughts. "This is Allen, IT specialist. What is your user ID?"

Allison replied with her hospital ID, and after a few seconds, the technician confirmed what she'd read in the email.

"This is crazy," said a bewildered Allison. "I just got to work, and I won't be able to do my job without access."

"I can't do anything about it tonight," Allen said. "Your account has been flagged for some security reason."

"And you can't get me on tonight, even temporarily?"

"No, I'm afraid not. This level of access denial must be handled by the department chief, and he isn't here until eight in the morning."

"Is that Andy Marchman?" Allison asked.

"Yes, that's who you have to see."

Furious, Allison thanked him and slammed down the phone just as Dave appeared at the desk. "What's wrong, Allison? Things going that bad?"

"I'm locked out of the computer system for tonight and can't get in until I see the IT chief in the morning. I'm going to have to get other nurses to let me use their computers to check my orders and meds. This is a total waste of time for me. I shouldn't have bothered to come in."

"I know it's a huge inconvenience. You can use the old paper assessment forms we still have around and just chart longhand, except for the meds and orders. I'll leave my computer on and stay signed in so you can check those," Dave said.

"Great," she said sarcastically. Her night started off bad and never got any better. It took over an hour just to check orders and give her meds, which were already late. Hoping that nothing unusual would happen with her two patients, she assessed them and began the tedious process of charting on paper. She never saw Paula the rest of the night or stopped to eat during her shift. Before she knew it, it was six o'clock, and the next shift would start rolling in within forty-five minutes.

Luckily, her patients remained stable and she got her work done, but not without a lot of excess frustration. By 6:45 a.m., her relief still hadn't arrived, and for once she was appreciative that Connie Gaston was consistently at least ten minutes late. At 7:00 a.m. Allison gave her report on her patients, and by 7:30 she was finished.

Now she had to hang around until eight for that idiot Marchman. Actually, she was glad she had to meet with him, Sean's text and warning about him were uppermost on her mind. She looked forward to confronting him in person.

Her anxiety and fears had evolved into determination, and Sean's death sealed it for her.

Before she left the unit, she sought out Paula, who indicated she was just finishing giving report. Allison waited for her near the desk. Ten minutes later, the two of them walked down the hall to the nurses' lounge. "This night sucked. How was it for you? I never saw you after midnight," Paula said.

"Tell me about it. After I left you, I couldn't get into the computer, so I had to chart by hand all night, plus use Paul's access to get meds and orders. Now I have to hang out until eight to meet that creep Marchman in IT. And I wanted to talk with you too."

"I'll be here late too. I have to meet with Bobbi this morning. I'll text you when I'm done, and if you're still here maybe we can go to breakfast or something. I'm so wired. I doubt if I'll be able to sleep. Plus, I'm off tonight."

"Okay. I'm heading downstairs to IT. If I'm lucky, he'll be in early."

Allison had a game plan for Marchman, and it included much more than getting her access reactivated. On her walk toward the IT department, she dialed Detective Derning's cell phone.

Chapter 19

Bobbi Herschfelt was used to getting by with little sleep, so it was no surprise that she was awake at four thirty this morning. She got dressed and made a banana smoothie before leaving her house for the hospital at seven o'clock. With traffic, she got to the parking garage by seven thirty. She stopped by the hospital cafeteria to grab a coffee and was in her office waiting for Paula by seven forty-five. She logged onto her computer and checked emails.

Ten minutes later, Paula knocked on her door.

"How was your night?" Bobbi asked as Paula closed the door behind her.

"Very busy, as usual. I barely had time to finish my work. And I never took a lunch."

Ignoring Paula's comment, Bobbi addressed her tersely. "You read the email I sent you. Do you know why you're here?"

"I guess it has to do with the email I received from Ethics," Paula said.

Surprised and suddenly more nervous than she already was, Bobbi leaned forward and asked, "You got an email from Ethics? What was it about?"

"About an inappropriate relationship with my immediate supervisor," Paula stated with a cavalier attitude and a hint of sarcasm.

"That is exactly why you're here. I thought this was behind us, but apparently someone else doesn't think so and notified the ethics department," Bobbi stated coldly.

"Don't look at me," Paula said. "Why would I do that? What I do on my own time is nobody's business anyhow."

"I received a notice from them about the same situation, and now they're investigating. Have you talked about this to anybody?"

"No, but people probably weren't naïve to the fact. I even heard other travelers talking about it when I worked down south after you left. You know how stuff gets around."

"Well, we need to be on the same page about this, because even though nothing happened while you worked in my unit, it doesn't look good that I'm your supervisor now."

"What do you expect me to say?"

"I expect you to say that it didn't happen. Plain and simple," Bobbi replied. "Otherwise, I have to transfer you to another department or fire you, and I can't afford to lose any more nurses. We're short enough as it is."

***

Paula couldn't care less that Bobbi was so worried. She knew she wouldn't fire her. "Well, if you fire me or move me to another department, I'll have a case for HR and will have no incentive to keep the truth from coming out," Paula said, fully aware that she held all the cards. She knew she could get a job anywhere, so the threat of being fired meant nothing to her. "Look, I don't care. I'll tell them whatever you want, but I need something from you."

"What is it?"

"This guy from IT, Andy Marchman, the director, has been hassling me and Allison too. It started before that Root Cause Analysis, and I think there's a lot more to it. For all I know he could be sending these emails himself to scare us. The other morning, I went out to the parking garage to find my tires slashed, and Allison had her car keyed. Plus, a threatening note was left in her locker."

"So why do you think he's behind this? What proof do you have?"

"No proof, just an educated guess. Any number of reasons, but he's a whack job and I don't trust him. He has it out for the SICU nurses, I think. He gave all of us a hard time when his mother was a patient. I remember what a pain in the ass he was when she died in our unit," Paula said.

"Then when Mr. Wetherly died, it was Andy from IT who conveniently uncovered unusual computer activity and made a big deal about it. We had to waste time in a stupid Root Cause Analysis."

"It was a big deal. A patient died," Bobbi said, glaring at Paula as she sided with her fellow administrative staff member.

"Too many things don't add up. Coincidentally, Allison is meeting with him this morning, because she was locked out of the computer all night with some bullshit story about computer security and inactivated access."

"I didn't know about any of this. Why wasn't I informed? If I don't know about it, I can't fix it."

"Well, what good does it do? Nothing gets done about it anyway, so people don't tell you everything."

Bobbi ignored Paula's criticism of her. "So we're on the same page then? You're not going to acknowledge the relationship we had?"

"I'm not going to say anything or even reply to the email. I think it's bogus. But I want something done about Marchman. He's creepy and dangerous," Paula said. "There. I've told you about a problem, so you can't say you didn't know about it."

"I'm going to reply to the Ethics email, promising them full cooperation and telling them it must be a misunderstanding. And I'll see what I can do about Marchman."

"Whatever," Paula said as she got up to leave, knowing the meeting was a colossal waste of time. A quick glance at her watch told her it was 8:20 a.m. On her way out of the hospital, she texted Allison to let her know she was ready to meet for breakfast.

***

Detective Derning's cell phone rang. He was preoccupied but answered the call anyway when he saw Allison's name on the caller ID.

"Good morning, Detective. It's Allison Jamison. I'm just getting off my shift and have some information for you."

"What is it, Allison?"

"I can't go into all the details now, but a lot has happened. I think you need to check out the IT director at the hospital. His name is Andy Marchman."

Derning suddenly was all ears. Marchman was already on his radar as a suspect in a hit-and-run MVA the day before. Straightening up in his chair, Derning said, "Allison, tell me what you know. I'm taking notes."

"I think he's been sabotaging me at work. All night I was locked out of my computer, and he controls our access. And I also have reason to believe he's the one who left that threatening note in my locker and slashed another nurse's tires."

"What leads you to believe this?"

Allison took a deep breath to steady herself before replying. "My ex was here doing some investigation of his own. He's a computer geek. He sent me a text warning me about Marchman and told me to tell you. He said he might be involved in Dr. Connolly's murder too." Choking back tears, Allison said, "He's dead. A hit-and-run yesterday."

"Allison, where are you right now?" Derning asked.

"I'm in the hospital cafeteria. I have to meet Marchman to get my computer access."

"Hold on, Allison. Wait for me in the lobby. I'm just around the corner and will meet you there in ten minutes. Do not go to his office. Understood?"

"Yes, I'll be waiting."

***

Andy Marchman had arrived at work early and was sitting in his office waiting for Allison Jamison. He knew she'd phoned the after-hours IT support line during her shift the night before. *It's the little things that make me happy*, he mused with anticipation.

His daydream ended abruptly, however, when his door swung open and two uniformed police officers approached him, escorted by Rob Chapman, the hospital CEO. Detective Derning also accompanied the officers.

"Orlando police. Andrew Marchman, you're under arrest."

***

Already tired, Allison hoped Detective Derning would show up soon. Instead, she spotted Paula strolling down the hall toward the lobby.

"Allison, what's going on? My meeting with Bobbi was over ten minutes ago. Why are you still waiting for Marchman? Where is that piece of crap?"

"It's complicated. I don't even know where to start. I called Detective Derning on the way to see Marchman, and—"

"What? Why? What happened?"

"Let me explain as quickly as I can, because he's going to show up any minute. I had to tell him Sean was dead."

"Oh Allison! I know it must be so hard." Paula hugged her friend and held onto her for a few seconds until Allison pulled away.

"Thanks. I don't know what to think. I'm so confused."

Paula cringed at the thought that an employee they knew could be a murderer. "I told Bobbi about Marchman, that he was creepy and about his targeting us."

"What did she say?" Allison asked.

"Not much, as usual. She said she'd handle it, but she might as well have said nothing. It kills me how some people get away with anything here. Not us peons, though."

"Yeah, tell me about it. Why don't you wait here with me and talk to the detective too, since we're both involved? I wonder where he is. He said he was just around the corner."

Critical Cover-Up

"So you seem kind of calm, even though your ex just died. I know you must still be in shock," Paula said.

"I'm just numb. First it was Joe, now this. Plus all the other shit going down at this hospital. I'm so disgusted. I wish I was somewhere else far away," Allison said, biting her lower lip. "Sean was a nice guy. We didn't talk often, but he offered to come out here to cheer me up and do some investigating on his own. He was suspicious of Marchman all along, I think. Since he's a computer geek, or was one, he knew how to hack into databases. I think that's how he discovered Marchman was monitoring us. I have so many questions and would like to get into his locked cell phone and computer. Maybe Detective Derning can check them out."

Just then, Allison heard her name and turned around to find Detective Derning standing nearby. He had a grave expression on his face, and his voice was devoid of emotion when he greeted her. "Good morning, Allison. May I sit down?"

"Yes, sure. This is my coworker Paula Fisher. She has something to share with you as well."

"You won't be meeting Marchman this morning," Derning stated bluntly. "He's no longer employed here."

Staring in disbelief, Allison couldn't process this information fast enough to know whether she was surprised, shocked, confused, or relieved.

"We just arrested him for the murder of Dr. Joe Connolly. That's why I told you to wait for me here. Sorry I'm late."

Allison's eyes welled up and she couldn't speak. She choked back the lump in her throat. Paula clung to Allison and didn't utter a word.

"So you wanted to talk to me? Do you have information about this case? Every detail is important," said Derning.

Regaining her composure, Allison pushed back her feelings and spoke in a business-like tone, as she so often had to do in critical situations at work. "Yes, I have information, but it seems anticlimactic now."

"No, don't say that. Tell me why you called me, Allison."

She took a deep breath and began the story, trying to summarize the main points. She showed him the text message from Sean regarding his concerns about Marchman. "Now he's dead. He was the victim of a hit-and-run yesterday. Did you hear about it?"

"Your ex was Sean McNally?"

"Yes. You know about the accident?"

"I do, but I didn't know he was connected to you. My investigators are on the case," Derning said.

Allison described the events that led up to the present circumstances, citing the suspected sabotage of her car and computer monitoring, as well as the deactivated computer access at work. Paula chimed in, explaining the episode of her slashed tires and events related to the Root Cause Analysis.

Allison continued. "What was strange was that the text never came through until after the accident. I think Sean wanted to tell me more. I can't get into his cell phone, but he had his computer in the car with him. He was using it to track Marchman, I think."

"You have my number, Allison. Call me if you think of anything else." He gave Paula his card and indicated for her to do the same. "I'll have my investigators check out Sean's computer and his phone, if you have it with you. I'll keep you posted if we find out anything else regarding his accident. I'm very sorry for your loss. Allison dug Sean's phone from her bag and handed it to Derning.

"Thank you," he said as he got to his feet and shook Paula's hand. "I'll be in touch."

By the time Derning left it was 9:00 a.m. "I still have to go to IT to get my access restored. I'm sure someone else there can handle it," Allison said.

"I'll go with you," Paula said. "I don't have an appetite anymore. Let's just go home after this. What do you think?"

"I'm too exhausted to eat. Let's do it another time."

Like the walking dead, the nurses trudged down the hall to IT.

Chapter 20

Word spread quickly throughout the hospital that Marchman had been arrested and charged with the murder of Dr. Joe Connolly. The SICU nurses were particularly interested in the details, although not much more was known at the time.

Bobbi received a text from the CEO informing her of the situation. "IT Director Andrew Marchman terminated, effective immediately. Charged with murder of Dr. Joe Connolly. Interim Director is Tom Gallicki." Stunned for a moment, it was a relief that she would no longer have to deal with him and his threats to her nurses. She fired off an email, forwarded from the administration, warning the staff not to discuss it.

This morning, SICU was crazy, still filled to capacity, with more patients in ER and PACU waiting for beds. Always running at least one nurse short, SICU was a challenge for even the most experienced RNs. Ethical conflicts, burnout, and workplace fatigue were commonplace in this ever-evolving field. The previous one-to-one or two-to-one patient ratio had grown to three-to-one, which was borderline unsafe.

Travel nurses rarely signed on for an extension of their contract due to the heavier-than-usual workloads at Orlando Memorial Medical Center. Still, a camaraderie existed among critical care nurses who are exposed to patient suffering, life-and-death issues, and workplace stress on a daily basis. Having to think on their feet and make instantaneous decisions resulted in this tight bond.

Even while rushing to complete their tasks, they communicated with each other in hallways and medication rooms or over their unconscious patients' bodies.

As she walked through the unit, Bobbi was aware of the hushed conversations about Marchman's arrest, a hot topic with the nursing staff. She ignored them as if she never heard a word.

***

Allison finally arrived home at ten o'clock after resolving her computer access issue in IT. Drained, she stripped off her clothes and took a long, hot shower, as if the hot water could rid her of the loss and pain of the last twenty-four hours. She threw on an oversized T-shirt and got into bed. She was physically exhausted but unable to sleep, her mind full of worry. *I should feel relieved that they arrested Marchman, but I don't. Something isn't right.* She could sense it. She wondered about Sean, sure that Marchman had something to do with his accident too. Worried that he might get out of jail on bond, she dialed Detective Derning's number.

"Hello, Allison. Did something happen?"

I'm sorry to bother you, Detective. I just can't get it out of my head that Marchman was somehow involved in

Sean's accident. I forgot to ask you earlier if there's a chance he might get out on bond," she said.

"There is no bond for a capital offense like murder. He's not going anywhere," Derning reassured her. "We have investigators and specialists who can get into his phone and computer. I'll let you know whatever we find out."

"I'm sorry. It's just that I don't know how much more of this I can take," Allison admitted.

"Get some rest. You'll be hearing from me."

But as much as she tried, Allison wasn't able to sleep or rest. Her life had been turned upside down. Gone were her aspirations of making a difference as a critical care nurse. The place where she felt important because she could be instrumental in saving lives was not what she had believed it to be. Her world was crumbling around her, and an overwhelming loneliness pressed in on her. She had no real friends, and Joe's death had left a gaping hole in her heart. Now Sean was dead too.

Wallowing in negative thoughts, she contemplated her life imploding and no one even noticing. *Maybe I should have died in that car accident. I would have been better off. How could I have believed that life could be good, that if I worked hard I could make a difference? It was all just bullshit.*

With limbs too heavy to move and eyelids that could no longer stay open, she eventually fell into a deep sleep.

It was four in the afternoon when Allison was awakened by the sound of her phone. It was a text message. Still groggy, she rolled over to see who it was from. Paula Fisher. "R U up? Call me when you get this."

She placed a call to Paula.

"Did you get some sleep?" Paula asked.

"Not much," Allison grumbled. "I'm still half asleep."

"Don't you have to work tonight?"

"I guess I do," Allison replied, "but I feel like calling in. My heart's just not in it.

"Listen, we need to talk. I never told you about my meeting with Bobbi."

"What was it about that was so important?"

Allison listened halfheartedly as Paula detailed the contents of the email she had received from the ethics department and the follow-up email from Bobbi. "A few years ago when I worked in Aventura, Bobbi and I had a thing going."

Allison perked up, hardly believing what she heard. "What are you taking about? A relationship?"

"Yes. It was pretty hot and heavy for about a year. I know it's hard to believe, but she was a lot nicer then."

"I had no idea she was gay. I thought she was divorced."

"She doesn't like to think she's gay, and now she got the same email from the ethics department and wants me to deny that anything ever happened between us. She sort of threatened my job in the unit, but she has more to lose than me," Paula explained.

"So what are you going to do?"

"I told her I wouldn't say anything, but I wanted her to take care of Marchman. I explained about how he sabotaged both of us. She seemed reluctant to get involved. Really, no backbone at all. I have totally lost whatever respect I ever had for her. She's just a puppet for the administration, a yes-person."

Allison sighed with relief, thrilled to know she finally had an ally. "Listen, I'm so disillusioned with that place.

I'm ready to do something that would make them sit up and listen."

"Forget it, girlfriend. Nothing would make them change. They are so entrenched in presenting an appearance that they've prostituted themselves on morals. That mission statement is a complete joke. What does it say? 'Quality and integrity is at the core of all we do.' Give me a break."

"I know, tell me about it. And they really think we buy into all that crap, when all they do is cover things up. And what about treating every patient with respect and equality? When they have a VIP, they expect us to double our workload so the patient can be assigned to only one nurse, when he clearly is a two-patient assignment or more."

"I know. You and I are definitely on the same page. I've been sick of it for a long time," Paula admitted. "But do you really think you can make them change or 'sit up and listen,' as you say? I think you're being naïve."

"I don't know, but I feel I have to do something. I'll call you later."

Allison ended the call, dialed the hospital number, and called in sick.

Chapter 21

Bobbi was on her way to a meeting when her phone buzzed in her pocket. She didn't recognize the name on the caller ID, but the number looked familiar.

"Good morning. How may I help you?" she said.

"This is Evelyn Beardsley in the ethics department. I need to clarify a few things regarding an email we received from you, supposedly in response to an email from our department. There are two issues of concern, including the subject matter of the email."

"What is the other issue?" Bobbi replied in a curt, business-like tone.

"The other is actually a more serious concern, that being the origination of the email. Our department did not send it to you."

"What do you mean, you never sent it? It's dated and clearly states the sender as the ethics department," Bobbi answered bluntly. She wasn't one to conceal her aggravation. *I don't have time for this nonsense.*

"Be assured we didn't send it, so that means only one thing: the system has been hacked. I'm contacting Rob

Chapman as soon as I finish this call. I just wanted to clear up a few things."

The CEO? That's all I need. If he reads the email, I'll be in for all kinds of questions. Frantic at the idea, Bobbi paused at the end of the hall to talk in an area with less noise and distraction.

"You indicated we'd have your full cooperation in this matter. Since we didn't originate the email, we aren't privy to the details. We'll need you to provide them."

Does this chick think I'm stupid? If she thinks I'm providing details, she's crazy. Bobbi realized almost immediately that this was her way out. Her ability to think on her feet during crises often served her well, and for that she was grateful.

In an almost sickeningly sweet voice, Bobbi replied, "You're right, I did say that, and by that I meant I'd be happy to answer any questions." The sugary tone quickly faded. "But the fact is, this claim is false. It's without any basis. There never was an inappropriate relationship with anyone. Whoever sent the email must have a vivid imagination, because they fabricated a story to create a problem."

"Are you telling me there is no truth to this allegation?"

"That's exactly what I'm telling you, so when you report the hacking situation to Chapman, you can pass the other information along as well." Bobbi had regained the upper hand, and she smiled, satisfied she'd avoided another catastrophe. "I'm late for a meeting. Have a good day."

She ended the call and continued down the hall toward her meeting location. She hadn't achieved her powerful position in the health care field without cause.

Hacking. Marchman. Maybe what Paula told me was bigger than I first thought. Oh well, he's terminated, so the problem should be gone too. Bobbi was a pro at the art of denial.

***

Invigorated now that Marchman had been charged, Detective Derning was more confident. This wasn't an airtight case, but the evidence they uncovered was enough to charge him with first-degree murder.

They'd lucked out when one of the parking garage security cameras near Connolly's car turned out to be active. The video playback revealed a tall, thin man firing a gun in Connolly's direction before slipping out of the frame. The man's name badge was blurry, but they'd been able to make out the IT department logo beneath his name.

Derning still believed a connection existed between Connolly's murder and the hit-and-run. Now he made this his priority. If he could link the two cases, he'd be more assured. Sometimes his optimism was warranted, but oftentimes it was not.

Derning called one of the investigators from the Traffic Homicide Unit and queried him about the Sean McNally case. "Has the Crime Scene Unit recovered a laptop from the car in the hit-and-run case?"

"Yes, sir."

"Good. Make this case a priority. I'll meet you at the department in thirty minutes."

Derning's mind was swirling. He intended to find answers and was eager to uncover whether Sean's cell phone contained anything more about his warning to Allison about Marchman.

Chapter 22

"So what do you have for me, boys?" Derning asked his two top investigators.

"You'll be interested in this, Chief. We got lucky. Forensics was able to match a paint sample from the rental car's damaged fender to Marchman's car."

"Good. That puts him at the scene. What about the victim's computer and cell phone?"

For the next hour and a half, Derning's investigators shared what they had uncovered from Sean's laptop and cell phone. Pleased that the investigation was progressing so quickly, Derning was keen on going over all the details.

Sean McNally's laptop turned out to be a gold mine in that Sean had recorded his findings in Word documents.

It appeared that he had been able to hack into the hospital computer before his death and found Marchman's account, where he kept personal notes in files.

Besides those files, Sean's email draft box contained what appeared to be an unfinished email addressed to a user named ajrn2014, most likely Allison Jamison.

Sean's investigation of Marchman uncovered several key findings, including lists of female nurses who were assigned to SICU. These lists detailed their work schedules and vehicle license plate numbers. Names associated with these lists included Allison Jamison, Paula Fisher, Bobbi Herschfelt, and a few others Derning hadn't heard of. He made a mental note to check them out.

Another file titled Monitoring Activity included a list of login dates and times, monitoring computer usage on the days those specific nurses worked. Next to Allison's and Paula's names were additional notes mentioning a patient name Wetherly.

"We also found this in Marchman's car," one of the investigators said.

Derning examined a small piece of scrap paper with something written in black ink. "Bingo." The paper contained the name Sean McNally and a series of letters and numbers. It appeared to be a password. Beneath it, the note included the model of a car and a license plate number along with two IP addresses. "Did you identify these IP addresses?"

"We did. They correlate with the cell phone you gave us and the laptop we found in the rental car registered to Sean McNally," stated the other investigator.

Derning observed that the handwriting seemed familiar. "Hmm. Hold on a minute," he said as he rifled through his bag for the envelope Allison had given him weeks ago.

He compared the latest note to the handwritten warning Allison had received, and the handwriting looked exactly the same. "Send these two to the lab for handwriting analysis, and tell them I need it yesterday."

"Got it, Chief." He was up and out of the room in an instant.

"Show me the email again."

The investigator complied, and Derning took his time as he carefully read the text of the unsent email Sean had written. "Allison, Marchman is dangerous. Found documents detailing your work schedule, social security number, email address and other personal info, like make and model of your car, where you usually park, etc. Same for Paula, Bobbi, and other RNs in SICU. Also found files with personal information about Dr. Joe Connolly. Am very worried about your safety. Send this info to Detective Derning as soon as you receive. I'll—"

He stared at the screen long enough to appreciate the gravity of the message. *How long had this surveillance been going on? And no one at the hospital ever suspected Marchman of anything?*

When the other investigator returned, Derning wrapped things up. "Great work, guys. We have to make this case airtight. Once we get all the loose ends tied up, we can charge him with the murder of Sean McNally too. What a scumbag."

Derning considered calling Allison but decided to wait. She wasn't in any danger since Marchman was in jail.

Chapter 23

Allison opened up a beer and microwaved a Lean Cuisine while her thoughts were far away. Her decision to take a sick day wasn't without cause, given the level of stress she'd been operating under.

She curled up with Snowball, her 12-year-old tabby, and ate her simple dinner on a TV tray. Cats were ideal pets. They didn't have to be walked, and they seemed to have an innate sense of when you needed a friend. Allison's tension melted away as the comforts of home embraced her.

Before long, however, thoughts of the hospital and its inherent corruption returned. *I have to do something,* she thought, *or I'm as dishonest as they are.*

She knew she had to devise a plan where she could expose the unethical practices yet maintain her nursing license. Nursing was her only source of income. Random ideas she had been considering were taking shape into a conceivable scheme. With Paula as an ally, Allison believed they could achieve her goal of making a real change.

She picked up her phone and called her friend. "Paula, I think I have the beginnings of a strategy that could work. I know you don't believe we can change anything, but hear me out, okay?"

"Okay, I'm listening."

"Remember when you told me administration planted patients in the units as spies from time to time?"

"Sure, they do it every six months or so."

"Well, I believe it. We're there and we see these examples of corruption and cover-up almost every day. And we've complained about it at staff meetings and mentioned it in our employee satisfaction surveys."

"Oh yeah, the ones they swear are confidential. What a load of crap," Paula said, laughing.

"Right. We all know that's bullshit. So instead of informing them of our opinions and believing they give a shit, we become the spies. We start taking notes every shift we work and keeping track each time they cover something up or push the rules to make them work in their favor. Our goal will be to disclose whatever illegal, immoral, or illegitimate practices we see going down. And include all the times the administration prioritizes their own interests over those of patients. How many times have we seen them give precedence to financial incentives and managerial values over safe patient care and employee satisfaction?"

"I like it a lot. Go on."

"We have to be discreet, not involve anyone else, at least at first. My aim is to do this for a specific time period, not more than six months, and then expose them for what they are."

"And how do you plan to do that?"

"I'm not sure of all the details yet, but I want to go public. Write a book and then go to the press, or maybe the other way around. I'll figure it out. Of course, our jobs will be toast at that point, but if we carefully plan it out, we can secure travel contracts so we'll have nursing assignments away from here without worrying about this place. I have nothing keeping me here."

"So we have to start thinking six months out," Paula said. "In the meantime, we'll collect as much information as we can. I already have current nursing licenses in California and New York. It would be a good idea if you apply for them now too."

"Great idea. I doubt we'll have any problem uncovering enough dirt in that amount of time. Shit, we already have plenty to start with."

Allison ended the call. Energized by their conversation, she got right to work making a list of all the incidents she could recall where either an attempt to hide something had occurred or unsafe situations had been allowed to continue. No longer trusting the security of her computer, she began her notes on her iPad. Later she would write the detailed story behind each incident.

Her fingers couldn't keep up with the rapid pace her mind was moving, so she closed her eyes and took a breath to compose herself. The memories whirled inside her head as she documented each one in no particular order. Cryptic at best, but she understood what each phrase meant: special treatment of VIP patients to the neglect of others; alcohol inside the hospital on New Year's Eve; supervisors leaving the hospital for hours while on the clock; telling staff to clock in and out for lunch when they had no time to take a lunch; reading instructions for equipment and signing off that you were competent; questioning the reason you called in sick; unsafe triple-patient assignments as a routine;

taking a nurse away and replacing with a tech. More to come.

Chapter 24

"You're getting a cardiac alert, Paula. Transfer Bed 7 up to stepdown. I have a bed for him," Dave said to Paula about an hour into her shift.

"You've gotta be kidding me. I already have three patients and just finished getting report. Now I have to move one out and get an admission?" Paula asked if someone could pack up the patient's belongings and get him ready to go while she called report.

"No such luck," Dave said apologetically. "Everyone has three patients already, and I have two."

This had become the norm. No room to breathe. No one to help because everyone was slammed already. It's not that they didn't have enough nurses assigned. The schedule looked good yesterday, but the directors had been told to tighten up their numbers, so they destaffed a nurse. *Makes a lot of sense. I can't believe they pay people to make these stupid decisions. Now SICU will work short, and everyone will have a miserable night. God forbid we'd have a shift when we weren't killing ourselves.*

At lightning speed, Paula called the stepdown unit and gave a fast report to the nurse who'd be getting her patient as a transfer. She packed up his belongings, grabbed his chart, and moved him upstairs in a wheelchair.

When she returned to the unit, her plan had been to quickly assess her other patients and set up the room once it had been cleaned. As usual, things didn't go as she'd hoped.

"There's been a change of plans," Dave said before Paula could put the wheelchair back where it belonged. "The cardiac alert is coming back from the cath lab with a balloon pump."

An intra-aortic balloon pump is a device often used to decrease the workload on the heart after a heart attack. The pump has an additional benefit of increasing blood flow to the coronary arteries, thus providing extra oxygen delivery to the cardiac muscle. These patients are usually made a one-to-one.

"I was able to get the supervisor to send me a nurse from MICU, and she'll take your other two patients once she gives report up there. Get everything done so you'll be ready for this patient."

Geez, it never fails. Musical beds. This all could have been avoided if administration hadn't told a nurse to stay home. "What about the nurse they destaffed? Isn't she on call?"

"No, it was one of the travelers, and they don't take call," Dave said.

"Such a stupid operation," Paula muttered. *Complete lack of efficiency. And then they wonder why the employee satisfaction scores are always low.* She made a mental note to add this situation to the list she and Allison were compiling.

"Oh, and by the way," Dave added, "this patient is Andy Marchman, the one arrested for Dr. Connolly's murder. He came in from the jail with chest pain and apparently was in the middle of a heart attack."

Paula's stomach immediately tightened like a knot and she protested the assignment. "I can't have him, Dave. I don't think I can take care of him without being judgmental."

"Paula, there's no option here. You're the only one who can take the balloon pump now. The other nurses who are credentialed already have three patients each. Besides, you're a professional, and he'll have armed guards with him from the jail."

This just sucks. I hope he's on a ventilator so I don't have to listen to his mouth. I should have called in sick like Allison did. She was the smart one.

Within thirty minutes the room had been cleaned, and Dave had directed someone to take the empty bed down to the cath lab for easier transfer of the patient. Five minutes later, the cath team nurse was on the phone with report. The patient had received two stents and was on a vent. *Thank you, God!*

Chapter 25

Exactly ten minutes after Paula received report, the cath lab team arrived with Marchman, the balloon pump at the foot of the bed as if it was attached. There had barely been enough time for respiratory therapy to set up the ventilator in the room before the patient arrived.

Paula and Dave worked side by side to get the patient hooked up to the monitor and admitted. The cath lab tech plugged in the balloon pump, which had been operating on battery for the transfer. Marchman's vital signs were stable at the moment, and his EKG looked okay. Dave noted the settings on the IV pumps which controlled several vasoactive drips. Two-armed Orange County Jail security guards accompanied the patient.

"Thanks, guys. We're good," Paula called out to the cath lab team. "Thanks for your help too, Dave. I'm okay now."

"Sorry for all the confusion earlier. These assignments are getting to be status quo around here. Believe me, I don't like it either."

"Yeah, good thing you're young and can deal with it, Dave. I'm not sure how much longer I'll be able to."

One guard took up residence just outside the room after asking for a chair, and the other made himself at home in the recliner in the patient's room. It always seemed ludicrous to Paula that money would be wasted on paying two security guards to watch over an unconscious patient who was tethered to machines. And for good measure, his ankles were shackled to the bed. All these guards did while they were there was eat and sleep. *Note to self: add this to the list.*

Paula had been a critical care nurse long enough to be objective and always treated patients with respect—two principles all nurses are taught to uphold. But some circumstances were more challenging than others. She would care for Marchman as she would any other patient, although she was grateful he was knocked out on the vent, and she intended to keep things that way.

The rest of the night was fairly uneventful. Before she headed home, Paula texted Allison, anxious to fill her in on the latest news about Marchman, but got no reply.

***

Allison woke early, eager to go to work to attain more fodder for her reconnaissance project. She noticed the text from Paula and sent back a brief apology for the delayed response before heading to the hospital.

As Allison got into her car, her phone rang. "Hi, girlfriend," she said. "What's going on?"

"You aren't going to believe who we have as a patient," Paula said.

"Tell me."

"Andy Marchman."

Allison stopped to catch her breath. "What? I thought he was in jail!"

"He was. He came in with chest pain. Apparently he was having an MI in jail. He was admitted as a cardiac alert, and the cath lab stented him. He's in our unit now, on a balloon pump. And Dave assigned him to me. Lucky me!"

"Oh my God! I can't have him. They'd better not assign him to me tonight. I'll refuse."

"They won't make you take him. You have reason enough to argue the point. I'll probably get him back. With any luck, he'll still be on the balloon pump and the vent."

"I guess we'll find out soon enough. Thanks for the heads-up, Paula. See you there."

Before Allison could return her attention to the road, the phone rang again. She was not surprised by the name on the screen. "Hello, Detective Derning."

"Allison, I have some news for you. Is this a good time to talk?"

"I'm on my way to work, so yes. It's as good a time as any."

"We were able to access Sean's cell phone and laptop and found a lot of information pertinent to Andy Marchman. In fact, we've tied him to the scene of Sean's accident."

Allison immediately perked up. "You mean Marchman is the one who hit Sean? He killed him?"

"It appears that way. We're going to charge him with Sean's murder as soon as he's conscious. You know he had a heart attack in jail and is in the hospital, right?"

"I heard about it. In fact he's in my unit!"

"That's what I understand, Allison. He's there with two guards from the jail. I want you to steer clear of him, do you understand?"

"Yes, don't worry. I don't even want to see that piece of shit."

"Good. I'll let you know more a little later," Derning said. "I'll be in touch."

Allison's mind was filled with visions of the accident. She imagined Marchman stalking Sean and then ramming his car and leaving the scene. Her eyes welled up, and tears spilled down her cheeks. Choked by sobs, she had to pull over because she could no longer see to drive.

Allison hadn't had time to grieve Sean's loss, but now she missed him and the sadness was overwhelming. She couldn't allow herself the luxury of embracing the ache in her heart, not right now, but she knew it was deep inside her. She found a Kleenex in her bag, wiped her eyes, looked into the mirror, and reapplied her lipstick. She took a minute longer to calm herself before pulling back onto the road. The drive to the hospital gave her enough time to regroup, and by the time she walked into the nurses' lounge she was focused on work.

At the desk, she checked her assignment and was relieved to learn that Marchman, who was still a one-to-one with the balloon, had been assigned to Paula. She'd gladly take her three-patient load instead of him any day.

***

Paula strolled into Marchman's room to get report and was not thrilled to discover that he was no longer on the ventilator and had been extubated. "Shit. Now he can talk," she muttered to herself. *He'd better not say one thing off-color or act like a smart-ass, or I'll put him in his place.*

Two new security guards were at their posts. As far as Paula was concerned, they were completely useless and just in the way.

Marchman was still shackled to the bed at his ankles, and it pleased Paula to know he couldn't get up. It was also a smart move from a medical standpoint, because the balloon catheter threaded into his right groin could become dislodged if he moved his legs, causing severe, if not catastrophic, bleeding. Paula had witnessed it once and didn't plan on it happening a second time in her career.

Chapter 26

Bobbi was still in her office when the night shift nurses arrived for work. She had stayed late so she could speak personally to each staff nurse that came on duty. Having already discussed the issue of Marchman with the day shift nurses, she approached the night shift RNs one by one as soon as they completed their reports, typically one of the busiest times.

Bobbi found Allison in one of her patients' rooms. "Allison, I need to speak with you. It won't take long."

Allison nodded and stepped outside the room.

"You know Andy Marchman is a patient here. Allison, I realize we all have our opinions about him, but I'm counting on you and the rest of the staff to treat him with respect and dignity, just as you would any patient. He's a former hospital employee, and we have to remember that he is innocent until proven guilty. Do you have any issues with that?"

"As a matter of fact, I do. If you recall, Paula told you not too long ago that he had threatened both of us."

***

Margie Miklas

Allison didn't want to mention what Detective Derning had revealed in his phone call, since she didn't know if it was public information yet.

"Yes, I remember, but we still have to treat him with respect, whether you believe he is worthy of it or not. We are professionals and that is what we do."

Why is she so determined to be nice to this guy? It seems like there is something more here. I wonder what her history is with him. "I understand what you're saying, but I don't think I could be impartial if I had to take care of him. So, as long as I'm not assigned to him, everything is fine with me."

Bobbi's tone made it clear this was not the answer she wanted to hear. "If you're a SICU nurse, you are expected to care for any patient admitted here," she replied curtly. "If you can't do that, we may have to consider alternate positions for you in the hospital. You do know there is a waiting list to work in this unit."

Oh please! Maybe there used to be. But by now the word has gotten out about the harsh working conditions, and the truth is, nobody wants to work in this unit. How can she be so naïve? They always seem to want to make you believe that they're doing you a favor.

"Yes, I understand. If I have to be assigned to him, I'll do my best," Allison said, telling Bobbi what she knew she wanted to hear, even though she didn't mean a single word of it. She had learned that being honest with Bobbi got you nowhere. *Another thing to add to the list, under the subcategory Sensitivity Issues and Favoritism.*

Allison walked back into her patient's room, signed in to her computer, and scanned her patient's orders and medication times before beginning her assessment.

***

When Bobbi approached Paula with the same message a few minutes later, Paula barely made eye contact, reassuring her that she had taken care of the patient the previous night and, as a professional, she could handle anything.

"By the way, you never heard any more from the ethics department, did you?" Bobbi asked.

"No, should I have?" Paula asked coyly.

"No, I think it's a dead issue."

Without batting an eye, Paula said, "I'm not so sure."

Bobbi turned and walked away, while Paula concentrated on organizing her nursing duties for her two-patient assignment.

A few hours into the shift, while she was caring for Marchman, Detective Derning arrived in the unit and stood at the door to Marchman's room. Paula recognized him from their recent meeting. "Hello Detective. How may I help you?"

"I'm here to see Mr. Marchman. I understand he is awake and lucid."

"Yes, sir. He's awake." Her interest piqued, she continued charting while closely observing the interaction between the detective and Marchman.

"Andy Marchman? This is your lucky day. You're alive and you are being charged with the murder of Sean McNally. Is there anything you want to say?"

"Not without my lawyer," Andy replied.

"Suit yourself. Looks like you'll be having a lot of conversations with that lawyer. Have a nice day." Derning walked out of the room, giving a nod to Paula. Once in the hallway, he said goodbye to Paula.

Margie Miklas

Holy shit! I wonder if Allison knows. I have to talk to her as soon as I'm done here.

***

Recalling that Allison was working that night, Derning asked at the desk where he might find her. "She's at that end," Dave said, pointing him in the right direction. "Try Room 4, 5, or 6."

"Thanks." Derning didn't have to go far before he found Allison in Room 6. She was listening to a patient's chest with a stethoscope. After waiting a moment, Derning cleared his throat and Allison turned around.

"It's official. We charged Marchman with Sean's murder. I just gave him the news. I thought you'd want to know."

"I don't know what to say. I have so many mixed feelings. I'd like to know more details, but I can't talk now, obviously."

"Yes, and I want you to know about our findings, the ones I can tell you without compromising the case. Are you off tomorrow? Maybe you can come by the station after you wake up?"

"I'm not off, but I can come by sometime after three. Is that good?"

"Sure. If I'm not there, call my cell, okay? And stay away from Marchman," he warned again.

"I will. Thank you, Detective."

***

Unable to process it all, Allison returned to her work and focused on her busy assignment for the next few hours.

When she caught up, she sought out Paula, being careful not to enter Marchman's room.

Paula stepped into the hall and the two allies quietly updated each other regarding Marchman's charges and Bobbi's weird warning to Allison about accepting patient assignments under threat of transfer. The shift ended without any further drama.

Chapter 27

After Allison awoke, she made coffee and had a yogurt before leaving for the police station. She was eager to hear the details about Derning's investigation. When she arrived at what had now become a familiar place to her, she entered and found Detective Derning at his desk.

"I got here as soon as I could," Allison said.

"The time is fine. I'm glad you could make it. We need to stop meeting like this," Derning said, trying to lighten the situation.

"So you said you found a lot of information on Sean's phone and computer?"

"We did, Allison. He definitely had uncovered evidence that corroborated what you'd suspected as far as Marchman spying on you and threatening you. We also found a partially written email that appears to have been meant for you. Is your email user name ajrn2014?"

"Yes. What did he say?"

Derning handed Allison a printed copy of Sean's unfinished email. He gave Allison time to read the words more than once. Then he cleared his throat. "Perhaps he didn't have a chance to finish it, but he was definitely sending you a warning and a message for us. I'm so sorry, Allison. Seems like he was a good guy."

Stunned, Allison sat quietly while tears filled her eyes and a lump formed in her throat.

"I can't divulge all the details, but this email was timed just prior to the 911 call we received after the hit-and-run."

"Was there anything else?"

"Yes, but I have to save some of that information for the grand jury and the rest of our investigation. You'll know all of it in due time."

"I understand. What about his computer?"

"Like I said, it's confidential, but Sean uncovered a lot about Marchman's hacking activities at the hospital. My investigators are still working on that. So for now we are keeping his phone and computer as evidence. Suffice it to say that you have a safer work environment now that he is no longer in charge of information security."

"Thank you, Detective, I appreciate this. Is that all for now?"

"Yes, that's it. Thank you for coming down. I hope this puts your mind at ease, at least a little."

Allison left the police station feeling exhausted but she'd manage, like so many other days when she'd work on limited sleep.

***

When she arrived at work that evening, she was surprised to find that Marchman was no longer in SICU. He had been transferred to the stepdown unit, her former workplace. *How ironic. Seems like eons ago.*

Paula was off, so Allison got right to work and, for a change, had a decent night. No one had been slammed with crazy assignments, and she actually had time for a real lunch break.

"I'm going on my break, Dave. I asked Melanie to keep an eye on my patients. They shouldn't need anything."

"Okay, Allison, Enjoy the rare occasion."

Allison left the unit and took the stairs up to the stepdown unit. She had already researched which room Marchman was in, and she made her way down the hall unnoticed. The guard seated outside the door was sound asleep. As she entered the room her heart skipped a beat, but she had an agenda, so the adrenaline was pumping. No guard was in the room, and Marchman appeared to be asleep. He had an IV in his right arm and was on telemetry so his heart rate could be monitored from the central telemetry desk in a room near the nurses' station. She observed that his ankles were still shackled to the bed.

Ignoring Derning's warnings, Allison spoke to Marchman. "So, Mr. Big Shot, you thought you'd get away with this and look at you now. Not such a big shot anymore." She could hardly believe she was confronting him.

He blinked rapidly, and it took a moment for him to realize who she was. He appeared weak and vulnerable, a far cry from the callous, bully persona he normally exuded. "What do you want?" he said.

"You can't begin to give me what I want," Allison told him. "You messed up and now you're going to pay. And I, for one, couldn't be happier. You made a huge mistake by screwing with nurses, in more ways than one. You'd better watch your back." Somewhat satisfied, Allison walked out of his room before he ever had a chance to reply.

Chapter 28

Allison was back in SICU in less than fifteen minutes and ate her Lean Cuisine in the lounge while mulling over her interaction with Marchman. He looked like a tired, beat-up guy lying in that hospital bed, yet he was a calculating murderer. It was all so difficult to process. She let her mind drift back to Sean and his unfinished email. He had tried so hard to warn her how dangerous Marchman was. The whole thing sickened her.

Once more she tried to put things together and figure out why Bobbi continued to protect him. She wondered if Paula knew anything. She'd call her when she was home later.

After she finished her lunch, she went back out to the unit, checked on her patients, and thanked Melanie for watching them. Both were stable, and for that she was grateful.

"No problem, Allison. It's good to get out of here once in a while. We don't do it nearly enough."

"Tell me about it," Allison said. *One more note to add to the list. They always insist we clock out a break whether we take one or not. It's ridiculous.*

She didn't see anyone else around, so she wandered to the other side of the unit and found the rest of the staff in Room 11. Apparently they had just called a Code 54, an overhead page for any available personnel to help subdue a patient who was out of control. She saw that enough people were in the room, with more coming down the hall, so she headed back in the direction of her patients. Before Allison rounded the corner, she was stopped in her tracks by the clatter of crashing metal, followed by yelling and frantic voices. She raced back toward Room 11, and couldn't believe what she saw. On the floor in the hall, a stainless steel pole lay toppled on its side with two double IV pumps and four IV bags still attached. The pumps' alarms squawked continuously, but she blocked out the shrill, annoying sound and hurried into the room. Despite the presence of five burly hospital employees, including a security guard, the patient was on his feet, gown off, and bleeding from what had once been an IV site in his left forearm. It seemed incredible that a critically ill patient could have enough strength to climb out of bed and cause such a catastrophe. One of the nurses arrived with a dose of Haldol, an antipsychotic drug which works fairly rapidly if given in a five-milligram dose. With the others holding the patient down on the floor, Allison injected it intramuscularly since there was no longer an intact IV site. *Thank God for drugs.*

ICU nursing is challenging and not only mentally stressful, but physically demanding. It's ideal for the twenty-something and thirty-something nurses. Yet the average age of an ICU nurse has continually increased in recent years. Today it's forty-seven or forty-eight. The level of experience of those nurses is phenomenal, and Allison wondered how they were able to keep hanging in there. Two of her coworkers had been nurses for over forty years and had worked most of those years in ICU.

After all the excitement, she went back to work and managed her assignment without incident. Her patients were good in that they didn't whine and weren't confused. Those types of patients were her worst nightmare. *Give me two vented patients any day. I'll handle them no matter how sick they are.* Being able to control their vital signs with IV drugs went a long way in managing their care, and Allison thrived on the control she felt in this climate. *Too bad I'm so disillusioned.* It had clearly become a dilemma, but she knew what she had to do. And she would bide her time, collecting evidence.

Once she got home in the morning, she texted Paula, who responded with a phone call. Allison shared her interaction with Marchman on the stepdown unit. "And do you know he only had one guard? It figures, two guards in ICU when he had his own nurse, and only one guard on stepdown where his nurse had five or six other patients."

"Yeah, that's the way they play the game at Memorial. Makes no sense. And let me guess; the guard slept all night?"

"Well, I don't know about that. I was only up there for five or ten minutes, but yeah, he was asleep then."

"Figures," Paula said.

"Hey listen, I wanted to ask you about something that's been bugging me. Since you know Bobbi better than anyone, why do you think she keeps protecting Marchman? She was as nice as pie to him during that stupid Root Cause Analysis. And she didn't do anything when you told her about the threats."

"You don't know why?" Paula asked.

"No idea. I've been trying to figure it out."

"You didn't know that he used to work at the same hospital in Miami where we worked? And he knew about us, her and me. Of course, I didn't care, but Bobbi was always paranoid. So once she realized he was here too, she steered clear of him as much as she could. But then when his mother was in here and he made life miserable for everyone, she had no choice but to see him every day. She was in that room kissing his ass instead of standing up for her nurses when he bullied them. Why do you think I lost all respect for her?"

"I didn't know, but that explains a lot."

"You're telling me. I knew those stupid emails we got about our relationship probably were generated by him and not the ethics department. But do you think I told her? Let her worry about it."

"He is such a piece of shit," Allison said. "I hope he gets convicted and gets the death penalty."

"I couldn't agree more. I have no doubt he'll be convicted. He'll get what's coming to him. And now Sean's murder too. I knew he was a scumbag, but two murders? And you went to see him and confront him?"

"I'm not afraid of him. He seemed pretty weak in that bed. And besides, he was still shackled at the ankles."

"I'll just be glad when his ass gets discharged back to jail, you know?"

"Me too. Hey, I've gotta get some sleep. Are you working tonight?"

"Unfortunately."

"Good, I'll see you there. Don't forget to take notes for our list."

"Don't worry. I already have a mental list going. I'll start documenting it in a file," Paula said.

"Okay. Good night," Allison said. She smiled, happy to have a friend in Paula. Things were beginning to come together.

Chapter 29

"Code Blue Room 538. Code Blue Room 538. Code Blue Room 538." The time was 6:15 p.m., nearing the end of the shift.

"I wonder who that is," Tracy said. "I hope it's not one of our patients we just transferred up to the stepdown unit." As charge nurse, Tracy left the unit to respond to the Code Blue. SICU nurses always dreaded the announcement of a code from their sister unit for several reasons. One, they had to respond to the code, even though the code team from ER also responded; and two, if it was someone they had transferred up there, it meant the patient had deteriorated. The final reason was that now they had to scramble to create a bed, since the patient would, in all likelihood, be coming back to SICU as an emergency transfer. Patient assignments had to be switched quickly, and usually some chaos ensued.

***

When the code team from ER arrived at Room 538, they found the patient's bed unoccupied. The door to his bathroom was open, and Maria, one of the stepdown nurses, and a security guard were inside the bathroom.

What they witnessed was a shock. Andy Marchman was hanging from the showerhead, a red biohazard plastic bag twisted tightly around his neck. His face was purplish-gray and his lips were blue. The guard and Maria were making attempts to untie the handmade noose and lower him to the floor without much success.

Two larger male nurses from the code team took charge and asked Maria to step aside. They held the patient's torso and lifted him enough for the guard to release him from the showerhead. They laid him on the floor and began the resuscitation process. After untying the noose and ascertaining that there were no signs of spontaneous respirations and no pulse, CPR was initiated and ACLS protocol was in play, with the ER doctor leading the effort. He questioned the team, "Does anyone know how long he's been down? Who found him?"

"I did," Maria replied. "I had a call on my phone from the monitor tech to check his monitor. I told him I had taken his telemetry off so he could take a shower, but I came down to check on him anyway and . . ." Terrified and flustered beyond words, Maria swiped the tears from her cheek and choked back a sob.

"This guy's a prisoner, and he wasn't shackled? Where was the guard?" the nursing supervisor queried.

"The guard was outside the room, and I had him unlock the shackles so the patient could take a shower," Maria said. "I thought he'd be okay."

The code continued for twenty minutes until all resuscitative efforts were exhausted. Despite the fact that the patient had attempted suicide, and that he'd been jailed with a charge of murder against one of their own surgeons, everyone in the room felt a sense of emptiness and despair when the code ended and they hadn't been able to save him.

"Time of death: 6:39 p.m. Thank you, everyone," the ER doc said, before he left the room to type a note into the computer. When presented with the code sheet, he scribbled his signature, and returned to the emergency room.

Tracy walked back downstairs to SICU, which by this time was buzzing with activity. The night shift had arrived, and everyone was waiting to see if the assignments needed to be adjusted.

Paula and Allison were checking their assignments and had only heard some rumors about an incident on the fifth floor. It was just a matter of minutes before word spread regarding which patient had coded and the ugly details about how it happened.

"You heard it was Marchman," Tracy told the nurses standing near the desk. "He apparently hanged himself in the bathroom. By the time we got there, he was gone. The asphyxiation caused by the compression on his carotid arteries would have deprived his brain of oxygen very quickly. Even if we'd been able to bring him back, he would have most likely been brain dead. He never had a chance. Now there will be a big investigation. I'm just glad it didn't happen in our unit."

"It couldn't happen here. Everyone is on a monitor," Karen said.

"Yeah, and he was supposedly shackled to the bed and had an armed security guard 24/7, plus telemetry upstairs too. Go figure. Bobbi's going to be a bear with this one," Dave replied.

Allison and Paula made eye contact with each other. "Do you believe this?" Paula said. She took some satisfaction in knowing that Bobbi would be stressed to the max. All Allison could think of was that he got what he deserved. She hated that bastard.

***

Within the hour, local news crews were outside the hospital getting ready to go live with the story. They were waiting for a spokesperson from the hospital with the latest information.

Dave, the current night shift charge nurse in SICU, had been briefed by the administration. Going around the unit to each of the nurses, he let them know that all the Os were in house—the CEO, CFO, and CNO—along with Bobbi Herschfelt.

"I wouldn't be surprised if they make rounds in here, so be aware. Nothing is to be said to any of the patients. We're still on lockdown, so there won't be any visitors for a while. I'll let you know more when we hear something. You know as much as I do right now. But since this is a high-profile incident, not to mention a sentinel event, maintain a low profile and just do your work. The news crews are out there, so try to keep your patients' TV sets tuned to *Jeopardy* or *Animal Planet* rather than the local news."

The unit was busy, so it didn't take much effort for the staff to focus on the patients rather than the big story. Admissions were lined up from the recovery room as well as ER. Before she could think too much about it, Paula noticed it was close to eleven o'clock. Since her patient remained sedated, Paula tuned the TV to Channel 9, the local Orlando ABC station, and texted Allison to come down to her room to watch if she had a minute. Together they listened to the reporter announce the details of a story they already knew.

"We'll keep you updated on this breaking story as more details become available," the reporter said as the segment ended.

Paula and Allison exchanged glances. No words were necessary as they went back to work.

Chapter 30

Bobbi had been on her way home from work when she got an urgent page from the CNO about a serious patient event on one of her units. "Fuck it. I can't ever get a break," she muttered as she made a U-turn to return to Orlando Memorial. She had no details other than the vague text message, but she knew it had to be serious if the CNO had already been informed.

She called the stepdown unit and asked for the charge nurse. "What's going on, Amy? I just got a page from Linda."

The skin on Bobbi's arms and neck warmed as she learned of the news. She was completely unprepared, and the anxiety increased a hundredfold. "How could that have happened?"

Amy provided Bobbi with a brief summary of the chain of events. Bobbi knew this major failure would be considered her responsibility, since it happened on her unit and policies were not followed. "I'll be there in ten minutes."

Plagued with anxiety, she mentally outlined her next steps. She knew risk management and administration would already be at the hospital. She was irritated at the thought that Linda would view her with poor regard because she didn't even know about the incident. *A director should be aware of what's happening in her unit.* If she'd heard this once in meetings, she'd heard it fifty times.

An inpatient suicide falls under the criteria of a sentinel event. And it wasn't that long ago that she had that RCA in SICU. *This is not a good day.*

Stepdown was a flurry of activity, above and beyond the usual everyday chaos. When Bobbi arrived, just as she had suspected, Risk Management Director Katharine Jenkins was there, along with CEO Rob Chapman and CNO Linda Steeling. This was going to take some time. As the situation demanded, Bobbi was in full management form and revealed no emotion. Two and a half hours later, she left the hospital without even stopping to look in on SICU. She knew Dave would text her if there were any real problems. SICU really ran itself, but she hated admitting it.

She bore no emotion about Marchman. She easily could have been glad that she no longer felt the need to protect him, but after so much time doing just that, she had become numb to her real feelings. The only emotions she seemed to be able to experience were anger and anxiety.

***

SICU was a madhouse. Almost all the patients were either really sick or crazy. It seemed to run in spurts; some nights most of the patients were confused, belligerent, and trying to climb out of bed. Such nights were more than frustrating for the already burned-out nurses like Paula.

It was close to 8:00 a.m. when she walked out to the parking garage, exhausted. Allison had already left, and all

Paula could think of was getting home, taking a hot shower, and falling into bed. She was tired of thinking about all the recent events at the hospital. Maybe it was time to think about finding another job outside the hospital. The only problem was that with her years of experience as a critical care nurse she was now making a high enough salary that few nursing jobs existed that could match it. The dream jobs, like working at an ambulatory surgery center with holidays and weekends off, just didn't pay enough. So it was continue on here and going through the motions for now.

***

Allison was already home, had showered, fed her cat, and was in bed when her phone rang. Caller ID indicated it was the hospital. Should she answer it? She wasn't on call, but her curiosity got the best of her.

"Allison Jamison?"

"Yes, who's calling?"

"Katharine Jenkins, director of risk management. We've spoken before, at a recent Root Cause Analysis."

Alarmed, Allison immediately became more attentive. "Yes, I remember. I just got home from work. Is something wrong?"

"Allison, you know about the incident that occurred last night on stepdown, right?"

"Yes, I was working, so we all knew what happened."

"I need to ask you a few questions, if you don't mind."

What could she want from me? That sickening feeling came over Allison, but she tried to sound as if nothing was bothering her.

"Okay," she said.

"Were you on the stepdown unit two nights ago?"

On hearing the direct question, Allison was stunned and wasn't sure how to answer. "What do you mean?"

"It's a straightforward question. One of the stepdown nurses mentioned that she thought she saw you going into Marchman's room in the middle of the night."

Her mind racing, Allison tried to think of how to reply. *I didn't see anyone. Who could have seen me up there?*

"No, it wasn't me. We never take lunch breaks. I would have had no reason to go up there." She lied, hoping her voice didn't give her away.

"Are you positive? We are investigating the death of a patient and have to cover all possible aspects."

"I understand," Allison said boldly. "I was in the unit all night."

"Okay, thank you. Sorry to bother you at home," Katharine said before she hung up.

Almost surprised at how easily she'd lied, Allison lay back on her pillow and closed her eyes. She felt justified in her actions as she thought of Sean and cried herself to sleep.

Chapter 31

"Can you believe that new traveler is gone already?" Karen asked Paula as they stood at the nursing station waiting for their assignments.

"That tall, skinny chick with the wild red hair and tattoo? I didn't hear anything. What happened?"

"That's the one. I think she lived on a boat at the lake. She got caught stealing drugs. She was asking people to waste narcotics with her but didn't show them the syringe, said she forgot. This morning when we were getting report, she was acting weird and laughing. She was so out of it that she fell off her stool. One of her patients denied that he had received any pain meds throughout the night, yet she'd scanned Dilaudid every two hours and charted that she had given it to him."

"I knew something wasn't right with her. I remember her now. I thought it was odd when she said she didn't know about Connolly getting murdered because she never watched the news. And she was always acting way too chummy for someone who just started here. Very bizarre. So did they get rid of her?"

"Yeah, they cancelled her contract and escorted her out this morning," Karen said.

"They should have called the police," Paula said.

"You know they'll tell her agency, and it'll be up to them. She'll probably be working in a hospital across the state in a few months and doing the same thing."

"It really sucks, and now we're screwed, since we'll be another nurse short."

"I know. It's the busy time already, so good luck getting anyone. Looks like we'll have all the overtime shifts we want."

"Great. Just what I want to hear. I'm too burned out already to even think about overtime." Paula mentally filed this away for her secret project with Allison.

***

This wasn't a good week for Bobbi Herschfelt. First a suicide and now another crisis which would make her life go from bad to worse. She didn't know how much more she could take.

One of her SICU nurses was discovered diverting drugs out of the Pyxis Med Station, the automated locked medication dispensing system. A major problem in hospitals over the past few years, drug diversion is the illegal distribution or abuse of prescription drugs or their use for unintended purposes. The hospital policy is very strict regarding partial doses of controlled substances, like opioids and benzodiazepines. The protocol calls for employees to "waste" any excess medications while being observed by another employee. Needless to say, the standard wasn't always followed. Sometimes the hectic hospital environment wouldn't allow for it. In other situations, employees felt insulted to have to watch a coworker physically dispose of the medication. And drug-abusing nurses would take what's known as the waste to use for themselves.

In today's economic climate, many hospitals have a tendency to place profits over patient safety, and Orlando Memorial Medical Center is no exception. Worse than that, though, is their tendency to cover up these serious patient safety problems. Much of what happens in hospitals flies under the radar, and one of the biggest issues is the matter of drug diversion.

With this issue so prevalent, a hospital's reputation could be on the line if the press were to hear about this type of situation. The hospital would be at risk of a lawsuit, decreased employee morale, and the possibility of even a greater staffing shortage. Since the bottom line is always money, the added expense of having to hire and train additional staff would severely impact the hospital's financial burden.

Despite the fact that stealing drugs is a crime, the state of Florida allows the practice of implementing the Intervention Project for Nurses, or IPN. This early intervention program is an alternative to disciplinary action. Nurses who adhere to the program are allowed to continue to work, agreeing to submit to random drug testing. Often they are allowed to work in areas where they do not administer narcotics.

The SICU nurse in question was a travel nurse who had only completed the first three weeks of her thirteen-week assignment. Since she wasn't a full-time employee, the hospital cancelled her travel contract and informed her agency. Now the unit was left short-staffed for the remaining ten weeks, as it was too late to obtain another travel nurse so far into the season. She was on the night shift, and they were already working with less than an adequate number of nurses. Another headache for Bobbi.

She wasn't looking forward to her meeting with Linda Steeling. She knew she was already in the hot seat for screwups in her units.

The nursing director was a short, heavy-set, middle-aged woman with fiery red hair. She was all business and didn't crack a smile when Bobbi arrived at her door. "Have a seat, Bobbi," Linda said tersely, as she pointed to a chair across from her.

Bobbi sensed beads of sweat on her forehead and was suddenly aware of an uncomfortable sensation in her stomach. For a moment, the thought of disappearing to a remote location, alone and with no responsibility, seemed very appealing. Reality quickly ended the illusion, and she made her best attempt at a pasted-on smile. "Thank you. Good morning."

"It's not a good morning, as you know. It's not been a good week. You seem to have lost control of your units. What is going on?"

Squirming in her chair, Bobbi took her best shot at an explanation, but she really didn't even believe it herself. "I admit it's been stressful. We have a lot of new staff nurses on stepdown, and they aren't really prepared to handle the heavy workloads." It was lame, and Bobbi knew it.

"What else?" Linda said, cutting her no slack.

"We've had a bad batch of travel nurses lately. They haven't been properly screened, and you end up with one like this one who stole the drugs."

"And isn't it your responsibility to screen the travelers? Last time I looked, it is one of the main aspects of a director's job. Not to mention the problem with your emails."

Bobbi was surprised Linda even knew about that. *That bitch in ethics. She must have made good on her promise to spill the beans to administration.*

"Listen, Bobbi, if you're having personal problems, you need to level with me. I can't have my director of critical care messing up like this. How do you think it makes me look?"

Worried about her own butt. That's all it is. She certainly doesn't care about me.

"No, everything outside of work is fine," Bobbi said. "I can get a handle on this. It's just been a bad set of circumstances. I'll meet with my staff and put some action plans together. I promise I can turn things around."

"I'll expect those action plans on my desk in the morning, and I'm giving you two weeks. That's it. Otherwise I'll be forced to relieve you of the position." Linda looked down at her computer, clearly signaling that the conversation was over.

Bobbi got to her feet. "Yes, ma'am. Thank you." She walked out the door, cursing under her breath, humiliated by being forced to thank the woman who'd just threatened her job.

Chapter 32

Allison's cell phone rang just as she was settling down to watch an episode of *Orange is the New Black*. It was Dave.

"Allison, I'm so grateful you picked up. We are extremely short because they had to cancel the traveler's contract at the last minute. Can you please come in?"

Allison knew they really needed help if he called. He was always so nice to her that she had a hard time saying no to him.

"How bad is it?"

"Bad. Everyone is tripled, and we have admissions waiting in the ER and PACU. If you could come in it would really help out," he pleaded.

As much as Allison had grown disgusted with the workings of her hospital, she liked her coworkers and still felt connected to the patients. "Okay, but remember this when I request a day off," she said with a chuckle, knowing it never really worked that way.

"Thank you, Allison. I owe you big time. How soon can you be here?"

"I need an hour," she said, figuring she needed to get some food together, change, and deal with early evening Orlando traffic.

"Okay, see you then," Dave said.

Allison was bored anyway, so she didn't mind going in. Besides, she could use the overtime money this week.

She fed Snowball and was out the door in half an hour. She was right about the traffic, one of the few negatives about living in Orlando. It was hard to believe that this city of close to two and a half million people had once been a sleepy southern town of less than 250,000. By 8:00 p.m., Allison had clocked in and was ready to work.

"Thanks so much for coming in, Allison," Dave said again. "You're a sweetheart."

Allison had to admit it did feel good to be needed. *Let's see how I feel in the morning.* She took report on two vented patients and got to work with her assessments, already an hour behind. Now that she had come in, the workload was a little less for the other nurses, so she felt good about that.

By 11:00 p.m. she was caught up. Her patients were critical but stable, and she had finished her computer charting and opened up her email. Most was junk, as usual, but there were two from earlier that day from Bobbi. One was titled "Urgent - Mandatory Staff Meeting." Upon opening it, she learned she'd have to stay another hour or so after her shift ended in the morning to attend the meeting. The good news was, she'd get overtime pay for it. The other email was titled "Policy on Drug Diversion." She wondered why she'd received this email, since she had just completed a competency on the topic. *Always overkill here. Do things in triplicate.* She'd read it later if she had time.

As she was headed to the staff kitchen to get a cup of coffee, Paula was walking toward her in the hall. "Hey, I'm surprised you agreed to come in. I know it's probably the last place you wanted to be."

"Actually, I haven't been doing so well alone. Just going through the motions. I hear that travel nurse's contract was cancelled. What happened?"

They both lingered by the coffee machine and continued their conversation. "You weren't here last night, so you didn't hear the big news." Paula shared the details about the nurse's firing with Allison. "What a loser. I say good riddance."

"Incredible that someone can work all night while shooting up narcotics," Allison said with a look of amazement on her face.

"Well, when you're an addict, it actually has the opposite effect. Dilaudid can make you feel energized and worry-free, even high. That's why it's one of the drugs abused most often by the medical profession. That and fentanyl, which is the drug of choice for anesthesia docs. It's so readily available."

"So I guess that's why we got an email about the drug diversion policy, right?"

"You got it, sister, and the sudden mandatory meeting too. I heard Bobbi's been a tyrant since all this went down. I'm kind of glad to see her so wound up. She deserves it after all the shit she's pulled," Paula said with a devious smile.

"When it rains it pours," Allison said. "I'd better get back to my patients."

"Me too. See you later."

***

Bobbi was up early and on her way to the hospital at 6:00 a.m. Still a complete ball of nerves, she weighed the idea of resigning over waiting to see if she would be able to placate her bosses enough to keep her job. *Do I want to be fired or resign with some semblance of dignity? And if I do resign, where will I go?*

The car ride in the busy early morning traffic allowed for some rumination, but nothing was resolved in her mind.

She'd just had a staff meeting with stepdown over the suicide of Marchman but gave the nurse a break, with only a written warning, and placed the majority of the blame on the guards from the jail. Other than a written action plan, which amounted to making a few changes in the policy, nothing was done. For some reason, she had a soft spot for newer nurses, but in this case, it was totally inappropriate. Someone had died, and the death could have been prevented.

***

The fact that Marchman's death solved one of her problems played into her actions more than anyone would ever realize. More cover-up and sweeping things under the rug for appearances' sake.

As for the drug diversion episode, nothing would make that look good. Her only saving grace was that it happened with a traveler and not a full-time staff nurse. Still, it reflected poorly on her hiring judgment and she knew it.

At exactly 7:30 a.m., Bobbi was in SICU demanding that everyone gather in the nurses' lounge for the staff meeting. Some of the nurses were still giving report, but she had no tolerance for that. So the majority had to leave what they were doing, and only a handful of nurses stayed in the unit.

"There will be another meeting tonight at 7:30 p.m., so any of you who absolutely can't make this one can come then. No excuses." Her authoritarian management style was front and center today.

The meeting began and Bobbi wasted no time getting right to the point, her primary focus on the issue with the travel nurse and abusing drugs. "I expect that all of you have reviewed the hospital policy on drug diversion. As you know, we have a zero-tolerance policy here on this huge issue. It's a widespread problem in this hospital and many others, but the fact that we had an incident in my unit is unacceptable. All of you have a responsibility to report anything suspicious. And if you know something and don't report it, you are at risk of losing your license.

"The travelers we got this time were not the smartest nurses, and we all have to keep our eyes open. It's just a good thing that none of you wasted any of her narcotic doses without seeing the syringe yourself, because that is grounds for immediate termination."

Karen spoke up. "I don't understand why it's grounds for termination if we don't speak up, when the person stealing and diverting drugs gets to go to a treatment program and return to work in a position where they can't dispense narcotics. All that does is make more work for the rest of us, while that person basically gets a pass. It's really not fair, and I, for one, resent having to do more work while someone else is rewarded, in effect, by doing less. They get to come back to an easier job, and we have to pick up the slack."

The rest of the staff agreed. Melanie said, "It isn't right, and if I have to give someone else's narcotics while they are skating by for abusing drugs, they are going to have to do some of my work. I'll give their drugs and they can give my baths."

The rest of the night nurses nodded, liking this idea, since they were tasked with giving baths in the middle of the night, even on alert patients. They had all voiced their opinions in previous staff meetings that this practice was stupid and definitely didn't enhance the patient satisfaction scores the administration was always so keen to see improved. Bobbi had heard it time and again.

She became impatient and expressed no sympathy for her staff. "Whatever you work out is up to you. I'm just telling you how it is. It's part of the Florida statutes that nurses who divert drugs have the option to enter the IPN Program and be allowed back to work if they have met the criteria. On to other issues."

Bobbi was all business. She didn't even have that fake smile plastered on her face. "You all heard about the incident on stepdown with Andy Marchman, the patient we transferred up there. No matter what you think about him, we dropped the ball on his safety. He was under the watch of a professional officer from the county jail, and he removed the shackles. We have reported this to the sheriff's department so they can further educate their guards on our policies.

"The nurse involved was new, and she didn't realize the gravity of the situation. But she was obviously devastated and even considered quitting over it. She was given a written warning. This occurrence was a Code 15, reportable to ACHA, the Agency for Health Care Administration, as well as a sentinel event that we had to report to Joint Commission. Luckily, none of you were involved.

"Obviously we need to talk about staffing, now that we are another nurse short after losing the traveler. If any of you want to work overtime, please sign up. We will approve all overtime while the hospital is at capacity. I can't do anything about the busy assignments. It seems this is going to be the norm from now on, so just be glad you have a job." For someone whose job was on the line, Bobbi was totally devoid of any expression of empathy.

"What about vacations?" Connie asked. "I put in for mine over a month ago and am still waiting to hear if it's been approved. I have to make travel plans."

"I will not be approving any vacations while we're this short. Administration would be all over me. If you can arrange something with your coworkers to cover you, I'd suggest you look at the schedule and see what you can work out."

Again, no hint of compassion for her weary, overworked staff. A few of the nurses looked at each other and shook their heads, and Bobbi noticed their unhappy expressions. As assertive as these SICU nurses were, Bobbi had total control and could end their careers in a moment. No love was lost between Bobbi and these nurses. She knew they had virtually no power but also realized they hoped her days at this hospital were numbered. Critical care directors had a history of moving on after three years or so, and Bobbi's time was coming.

***

Allison and Paula were both disgusted. Bobbi's tone and words only validated their frustration with the status quo. Nothing was changing and it was clear that nothing would ever get done. The culture of corruption and cover-up and more meaningless action plans had only worsened. They knew they needed to step up their plan of attack.

Chapter 33

"Code Blue SICU. Code Blue SICU. Code Blue SICU." Allison had just walked through the employee entrance to clock in for her next shift when she heard the overhead announcement by the robot-like hospital operator. The night was starting off with a bang. She took her time opening her locker and getting ready for her shift. It was only 6:38 p.m., so she was a little early. "No sense getting to work any sooner than necessary," she mumbled. Before she was finished, another announcement blared out of the speaker in the nurses' lounge. "Cancel Code Blue."

Someone probably pressed the red code button behind the patient's bed by accident. Visitors do it all the time thinking it's a light switch. *Oh well, at least the chaos will be less. What I don't need is any more turmoil and drama in my life.*

Halfway through her shift, Allison took a few minutes to catch up on her charting. Karen and Melanie were working nearby, and Allison struggled to block out their conversation until the words *oral sex* and muffled giggles got the best of her.

"What are you two talking about?" she asked Karen, who snuck a quick look at Melanie before both women burst out in laughter.

"You haven't heard?" Karen said. "The whole hospital knows about it. You know Jeff from physical therapy, right?"

"The tall guy who's always talking loud and thinks he knows everything?"

"Yeah. Tall, bald, and has a beer gut."

"Yeah, what about him?" Allison said.

Karen continued. "Apparently he had been dating a nurse in one of the other units. NICU, I think. Anyhow, he was giving her oral sex, and she took a picture of him with her freaking cell phone while he was going down on her." Melanie and Karen could hardly contain their laughter.

"Ugh. I can't even imagine how anyone would want to do it with him. He's beyond disgusting." Allison wrinkled her nose and grimaced.

"Really, right? And who grabs their cell phone in the throes of an orgasm anyway? It couldn't have been that good, that's for sure," Karen said, smiling.

"So what happened?"

"Well, I guess the chick is married, and the dumbass left the picture on her cell phone, and her husband found it. Of course, he went ballistic, but the dude decided to print the pic and make 8x10 black-and-white copies, which he attached to every car windshield in the employee parking lot at the hospital. How is that for revenge?" Melanie and Karen cracked up, and Allison grinned too.

"You're effing kidding me! That is unbelievable. How mortifying!"

"And that's not all," Karen said. "Listen to this. Administration got wind of it and contacted HR, because they were concerned that the husband could pose a threat and might come back and do something violent. So they called both of them in and threatened them with their jobs. We don't know what happened to the chick, but now Jeff is no longer working in any of the critical care units. So embarrassing."

"I wondered why I hadn't seen him lately," Allison said. "Thank God he isn't working in here, because the minute I see him, I know I'll have a visual of that disgusting scene. Ugh. I bet Bobbi is happy this wasn't one of her units."

"Isn't that the truth?" Karen said. "She just got lucky on this one. It's been one cluster fuck after another for her. She has enough to deal with. It wouldn't surprise me if she resigns."

"We'll have to see. She's blaming us for things that are clearly due to her own poor management," Allison interjected with no sign of empathy for their boss. "Wow, thanks for the laugh, ladies. I need to get back to my charting, but it was definitely a good diversion."

Wouldn't the public cringe if they knew what really happened in hospitals? They are about to, once we publish all this nonsense. Allison continued her charting, secretly smiling to herself.

Chapter 34

Allison sipped her coffee, relishing the few hours to herself before she had to leave for work. Snowball was curled up on her lap, and Allison was comforted by her steady purring and soft fur. The ringing of her phone startled her. She was surprised when the caller ID revealed it was Detective Derning. She hadn't talked to him since before Marchman died and wondered what this call was about.

"Allison, Detective Derning. How have you been?"

"About as well as can be expected. Not the best, but not the worst either."

"I just wanted to touch base and let you know a few things. You know we charged Marchman with Sean's murder, but since he died, the case is obviously closed. I just wanted to be clear. Also, I thought you'd like to know that my department was able to locate some family of Sean's in California. They made arrangements with a local funeral home to send his ashes to them. The family wasn't interested in any personal effects. I wondered if you wanted his cell phone and computer."

Allison needed a minute to process the information. "Oh, I'm glad you found some family. Who was it, if I might ask?"

"Some second or third cousin, I think. Her name is Mary Ann. You were right in that he didn't have a wife or children."

"I don't recall Sean ever mentioning her. But I would be interested in having the computer and cell phone, Detective. I appreciate you thinking of me. Should I come by the station to pick them up?"

"No need. I can drop them off. When is a good time, either today or tomorrow?"

"I have to leave for work by six o'clock, so anytime today between now and then, I guess," Allison said.

"Okay. I'll stop by around five thirty."

"Perfect. See you then. Thank you again."

The conversation about Sean and his ashes jolted Allison into a sense of profound sadness as she realized that she hadn't really grieved for him. Her mind retreated to the year they were married and how much fun they'd had together. Life was simpler then, when neither of them had any real responsibilities. They'd listen to music by Matchbox Twenty and Nickelback, and life couldn't have been any better. They were young, excited, and full of passion and love for each other. She wished that time had never ended.

The doorbell rang not long after Allison had finished getting dressed and packed some food for work.

She peered through the peephole before opening the door. "Please come in, Detective. It was nice of you to bring over Sean's things."

"I'll just stay a moment. I'm happy to do it, Allison. I'm sorry the way things ended up."

"Yeah, so am I. Have a seat, Detective. I have a few minutes before I need to leave."

"Okay. We did uncover some disturbing information on the computer and his cell phone that we might have been able to use if the case had gone to trial. Since these were notes and messages Sean made while investigating events related to you, I thought you might want to read them when you have some down time. So I'm leaving these with you, and they're both unlocked. I'll be going now, Allison. You know you can always call me."

"I know, and thank you very much, Detective. I appreciate everything you've done." Allison locked the door once the detective left. She sat down on the recliner and stared into space, numb, her mind a blank page.

***

Shifting gears once she arrived at work, Allison was all business. She received her assignment and began assessing her patient. God must have been smiling on her, because she only had one patient—a sick one, for sure, but she'd rather have a critically ill, unstable patient where she could best apply her nursing skills. She'd stay in her patient's room most of the night to constantly monitor and manage her care.

The patient was a forty-two-year-old Caucasian woman who had overdosed on fentanyl, a drug once used only in hospitals and then in prescription pain patches. Today, it's one of the most popular street drugs in the Orlando area. Allison had seen quite a few patients who had overdosed on this dangerous drug. Fentanyl is considered to be about a hundred times more potent than morphine and fifty times stronger than heroin. Sometimes heroin is laced with fentanyl, amplifying the potency of the fentanyl, making the effects even stronger. Orange and Osceola counties currently have the highest death rates in the state for fentanyl overdoses.

The patient was a one-to-one because she was unstable, on numerous IV drips, and on a ventilator. Her kidney function was marginal, and the plan was to start CRRT that evening. CRRT, or continuous renal replacement therapy, is a form of dialysis used when acute kidney injury occurs in critically ill patients. A vascular surgeon was on his way over to insert the vascular catheter needed to initiate the dialysis. The adrenaline was flowing, as Allison enjoyed this kind of challenge. She'd take this type of assignment any night over three confused patients trying to climb out of bed.

She needed a night like this, when she felt like a critical care nurse again, making a difference. Aware that her patient might not make it, Allison focused all her energy toward maintaining an adequate blood pressure for her with Levophed. *You never know in these early hours. I've seen patients turn around despite the odds. That's why I do this.*

By 2:00 a.m., her patient had been on CRRT for four hours and, although unstable, was maintaining a pressure and producing some urine, thanks to Allison's careful tweaking of the IV drips and dialysis flow. She hadn't stopped working since her shift began, and when her charge nurse stopped in to check things, she knew she needed a bathroom break. "Hi, Dave. So far so good here, but she's barely holding her pressures. Can you keep a close eye on her while I take a ten-minute break? I'm starving and really need to pee."

"Sure, Allison. How much Levo is she on?"

"I have her up to ten mics. I've been titrating up and down, just one mic at a time. She's very volatile and sensitive to any changes. I've been lucky to keep her mean right around sixty."

"Okay, take your break. I'll keep an eye on her."

"I won't be long."

Allison knew she wouldn't stay out of her patient's room too long. She headed straight for the bathroom and then grabbed her lunch from the fridge in the nurses' lounge. When she hurried to the kitchen for a cup of coffee, she found Paula standing at the sink.

"I haven't seen you all night. I know you're busy with that overdose. How is she?"

"Unstable and her pressure is very transient. I'm constantly having to adjust the Levo. How's your night going?"

"Wild. I have three patients. One is on the call bell every five minutes; one is just crazy, and the other one is constantly trying to get out of bed. If I wanted to work in a psych unit, I would have applied at University Behavioral Center."

"Tell me about it. What happened to the days when we had only post-ops in here and no three-patient assignments?"

"You can forget about those days. They are long gone. Hey, if I get a chance I'll stop by your patient's room. I had an interesting conversation with Dr. Chandra, the hospitalist."

"Sounds good, Paula. You know where to find me." Allison gulped down the last few bites of her lunch, tossed her Styrofoam coffee cup in the trash, and hurried back to resume her duties. Her patient's life depended on it.

Chapter 35

Bobbi stared at the near-empty bottle of Pinot Grigio. A bag of Tostitos chips on the nearby table was almost empty. It was ten p.m., and she had been on the couch since she got home at seven thirty. Still in her work clothes, she hadn't eaten anything substantial. She was disgusted with everything—her job, her life, herself.

If I died today, no one would even care. I've been prostituting myself for that hospital, and no one gives a shit what I do. They'd all be glad to get rid of me. They'd replace me without even feeling bad.

With much effort, she sat upright and filled her wine glass with the remainder of the Pinot. She hurled the empty bottle across the room toward the trash can at the edge of the kitchen. It missed by inches, crashed onto the ceramic tile floor, and shattered into smithereens. The thought of getting up to find a broom was more than she could bear.

Too drunk and exhausted to think straight, Bobbi closed her eyes.

At 5:30 a.m. the shrill sound from her phone woke her with a text message from Dave. "Urgent. Staffing problems this a.m. Call ASAP."

She sat up and realized that she had never removed her clothes, showered, or gone into her bedroom to sleep. Then she saw the shards of glass all over the floor. Her head pounded. "Shit. This is the last thing I need." She knew she had to move and prepare to leave for work but couldn't quite get her body to cooperate. She texted back, "Tell me the numbers. Patients and nurses."

Two minutes later, she received a reply. "The unit is full. 16 patients, 3 1-1s and 7 RNs. Two callouts."

Bobbi decided to call Dave rather than continue texting. The gist of the conversation was that the supervisor had no one else to send since there were callouts all over the hospital. "Did you try calling in staff?"

"Yes, everyone is burned out from overtime. We called everyone who isn't already scheduled and left messages. No one returned the calls. Nobody wants to come in under these circumstances."

"Do you think any of the night nurses would be willing to stay until eleven? Maybe by then we could get someone to come in."

"I don't know, but I'll check and text you back."

"Okay, Dave, and thank you." More stress and Bobbi was not handling it well. She wanted to crawl into a hole and never come out. She'd only felt like this once before, and that was when her husband announced that he wanted a divorce. She forced herself to abandon those thoughts as she waited for a notification from Dave.

After what seemed like a huge amount of time, Bobbi's phone alerted her to another text message from Dave. "It took some doing, but Karen will stay till 11."

Relieved, Bobbi texted back, "Great. Please tell her thank you for me." Energized by this short reprieve, she showered and dressed for work. By 6:45 a.m., she was headed toward the hospital. Resigning was no longer on her agenda.

Chapter 36

Allison got out late because her patient was unstable and the complex shift report took longer than usual. She felt a sense of accomplishment just by keeping her patient alive through the night. By the time she walked to the parking garage, it was after eight. Paula was long gone.

Once she was in her car and on the highway, she called Paula's cell phone. "Hi, it's me. I'm just getting out."

"I figured you'd be late. I'm already home. What's up?"

"You got me curious earlier when you mentioned talking to Dr. Chandra. What happened?"

"Oh that. Yes, you'll find this quite interesting. I think we should include it on our list of failures, cover-ups, and unsafe practices."

"I'm listening," Allison said with renewed curiosity.

"We were talking at the desk. You know he's leaving soon, right? He told me why he'd decided to go and how totally disgusted he is with the place. Apparently, these hospitalists have to document how much time they spend doing an initial patient assessment and history. It's all in the electronic record, and they are awarded points somehow, depending on the amount of time they spend with each patient. The points translate into money."

"Yeah, I know how that works."

"Well, on numerous occasions—in fact, more often than not—the hospital actually decreases the points. Say, for example, the points add up to a five. The hospital will change the value to a three, so they don't have to pay the doctors as much. And that's not all. He told me that when he first arrived, it took ninety days before he ever saw a paycheck."

"So the nurses aren't the only ones getting the shaft. They're screwing the doctors too."

"Exactly. He's had it and handed in his resignation. And to add fuel to the fire, they refused to accept it. Told him they can't let him go, even though his contract is up."

"How can they do that?"

"Who knows, but obviously they can and they did. And now he's afraid to leave, because he doesn't know if they're going to hold the pay he's due or what. He's so over it and really in a bind."

"That hospital sucks. All they care about is money, and the CEO always gets a fat bonus. Everyone knows that, and all they can give us for a raise is a lousy one percent."

"I know. I think we picked the wrong career. Have you started documenting anything for our report? I already have a list going with about fifteen incidents."

"Good," Allison said. "I have it in my head, but I'm going to make a point to get it on the computer. When are you off next? Maybe we can get together and collaborate to get this project moving forward."

"I'm off Sunday and Monday," Paula said.

"Okay, good. I have Saturday and Sunday off. Let's get together late Sunday afternoon. We can meet at my condo to work on it, set some deadlines, and then maybe go to dinner. I'd really like to get a lot of this pounded out and have a time frame for going public with the information."

"Sounds good. Call me."

Allison arrived home, and after she showered, was tempted to see what she could find on Sean's phone, but it would have to wait. Drowsiness caught up with her. She got into bed and was asleep within five minutes.

Chapter 37

When Bobbi arrived at the hospital, she went straight to SICU to see what was going on, now that the day shift had started. Tracy was in charge and things were hopping.

"Tracy, good morning. What's going on? Have you been able to get in touch with any of the day nurses to see if someone could come in at eleven?"

"I haven't had a chance. None of them answered their messages, so I doubt anyone will come in. I was hoping maybe we could get a nurse from another unit."

Somewhat refreshed and with an improved attitude, Bobbi replied, "Let me check with my other units, and I'll see if I can get someone."

Before Bobbi could reach her office, she was alerted to a text from Linda Steeling, the CNO. Terse and to the point, it read, "Meeting with me at 9:00 a.m. My office."

Great. I wonder what this is about. Bobbi's pulse quickened, and by the time she reached her office, a burning pain shot up the back of her neck. *It's not going to be a good day.*

She sat down at her desk, turned on her computer, and called MICU. She lucked out. An extra agency nurse had shown up even though she wasn't scheduled, and she was on already her way down to SICU. "Thank you, God," Bobbi muttered.

She perused her emails and replied to the important ones. Afterward, Bobbi left her office and made her way to stepdown to check on her staff. Two minutes later she was back in the hall, heading in the direction of the administration wing of the hospital. She didn't have a good feeling about this meeting.

She arrived at Linda's office to find he door ajar, the CNO busy at her desk.

"Come on in, Bobbi" Linda said as Bobbi raised her hand to knock on the doorframe. "And close the door, please."

Definitely not good.

"Please sit down," Linda said.

Bobbi took a seat. "Thank you," she said, though gratitude was not the emotion she was feeling at the moment.

Linda was all business. "As you know, your departments have had a lot of problems in the past few weeks, and the CEO isn't happy about it. Quite frankly, I'm not either. You've had an opportunity to clean up your act, but it hasn't happened. You haven't been able to control your units, and we can't have that. So I'm sorry to have to tell you, but you are being relieved of your position as critical care director, effective immediately."

Stunned, Bobbi had no idea what to say. She certainly didn't expect this. She had been in this role, killing herself for the hospital, for the past four years. And she thought she'd been doing a good job overall. Hell, she'd even lost a marriage over it. "I don't know what to say. I've been managing as best I could, given the circumstances with the budget and tight staffing and everything."

"Well, in reality, you haven't. Your employee satisfaction scores are among the lowest in the hospital, and the incidents in your units are more than what we can call acceptable. Not to mention your questionable ethics violations, which we aren't even going to discuss, as there is no need now."

So they did know about that email from the ethics department. "So, what is my status then?"

"I'll expect your letter of resignation on my desk by noon today. That will give you time to clean out your desk. Take your things with you as you leave the building. I'm sorry, Bobbi, but I have no other recourse."

"I'll be by in a couple hours with my letter," Bobbi replied in a stoic, business-like voice. She stood up and left Linda's office. She had never been fired before and could hardly think straight. She slipped into the nearest stairwell and walked up the two flights of steps to her office, hoping she'd avoid contact with other hospital personnel she knew.

Luckily, she managed to reach her office unnoticed, closing the door behind her. "That bitch," she said to herself. "So two-faced. Always acting like she had my back."

Sweat trickled down the back of her neck, and her head pounded. "I am so angry I could scream!" Knowing she had to suppress her feelings, she grabbed an empty box from the closet and cleaned out her desk drawers as quickly as she could. She only took the personal items and left everything else.

She logged back onto her computer to compose her resignation letter, staring at the screen for a minute as she figured out where to start. She certainly wasn't going to thank the hospital for the wonderful years and great opportunities they'd provided. No, she was bitter now and didn't give a shit.

Bobbi knew better than to burn her bridges. She kept it short and simple, adding none of the negative comments that might come back to bite her in the ass.

> "Attention: Linda Sterling, CNO, Orlando Memorial Medical Center
>
> This letter is to inform you that I am resigning my position as director of critical care at Orlando Memorial Medical Center. I am also ending my employment at the hospital, effective immediately, in order to pursue new responsibilities and challenges.
>
> Sincerely,
> Bobbi Herschfelt"

She smiled, taking particular pleasure in the last part, as she attempted to leave with some sense of dignity. She clicked Print, made two copies so she could keep one for herself, and grabbed the letters from the printer before logging off and shutting down her computer. The thought of deleting emails or uploading any documents to a thumb drive never occurred to her. After one final look around, she picked up the box with her possessions and walked out of her office for the last time, taking care to avoid eye contact with anyone in the hallway as she made her way back to the CNO's office. The door was open, but the office was vacant. Bobbi walked inside, left the letter on

Linda's desk, and walked out of the hospital for the last time. It was 11:35 a.m.

Chapter 38

SICU was hectic. The normal busy atmosphere had escalated to the next level. Patients were waiting in the ER and PACU for bed assignments, the staffing was tight, and the patients' acuity levels were higher than usual. The staff barely had time to accomplish the minimum tasks and provide care for the ever-changing critically ill patients. Tracy was at the end of the hall helping one of the junior nurses with a patient. When she looked up, she noticed the CNO walking into the unit with her assistants. It never failed that on days like this, the administration would stop in for an unannounced meeting with the staff.

With an entourage of two, CNO Linda Steeling walked toward the nurses' station, all smiles.

"Hi. How is everyone doing today? Who's in charge?" she asked, wearing a phony Cheshire-cat-like grin.

"Tracy's the charge nurse. I think she's helping in one of the rooms down the hall. Oh, there she is," one of the travelers said, pointing the CNO in the right direction.

Linda walked through the unit until she reached Tracy. "I'd like to have a little meeting with your staff. Can you ask them to gather around the desk?"

As inconvenient as it was, no was not an option when administration decided to call a meeting. Tracy was not happy, but she had worked in middle management at the hospital long enough to realize that this was standard operating procedure. "Okay. Everyone's really busy, but I'll see how many I can find."

"It will only take a few minutes," Linda said. Her minions, who were also wearing fake smiles, nodded.

Tracy walked through the unit, and within three minutes had managed to locate six of the RNs and directed them to the nursing station, where Linda and her underlings were now waiting.

"Good morning, everyone. Oh, I guess it's afternoon by now," Linda said with a grin, as if this were a casual conversation with friends. None of the nurses said a word. "I know you've all been busy and working short-staffed. I understand how hard it's been for all of you, and we are trying to remedy the situation. We really do care about you, but it might get a little harder before it gets easier. We are trying to negotiate with some additional travelers for your unit, but it will take some time. You are all doing a fantastic job. We want to thank you for all that you do every single day."

Tracy noticed some of the nurses exchanging quick glances. How often had these seasoned nurses heard this same speech, as though these phrases were talking points learned in Leadership 101?

"What I wanted to share with you today, though, is something serious that will impact your unit immediately. I want you to be the first to hear that I accepted your director's resignation this morning. I am not at liberty to discuss any of the details, but suffice it to say that she is gone and will not be returning."

Everyone looked around at each other in silence—wide-eyed, mouths open, and heads shaking in disbelief. One nurse mouthed the words, "Oh my God."

Linda continued. "We will be posting the position immediately and likely will be hiring a director from outside the hospital. In the meantime, I will be acting as your interim director. I know your unit functions fairly independently, and I trust that you will all do your best to continue on. If anyone wants to sign up for overtime, we welcome it, especially while we're so short-staffed. I am giving your charge nurses the authority to approve all overtime for the next month. Any questions are to be referred to your charge nurses, who are free to contact me at any time.

"Thank you for continuing to be the best critical care nurses you can be. I have every reason to believe that all of you will rise to the occasion, and we will get through this challenging time together. Have a good day, everyone."

That was it. No time for questions or other comments. Within three minutes, Linda and her associates in white coats were gone.

Tracy looked at her staff with resignation and shrugged. "I honestly had no idea Bobbi was leaving," she replied to the nurses' quizzical expressions. "I know as much as you do. I guess we're sort of on our own, like we have been anyway. So, carry on. Oh, and about the overtime . . . look at the schedule and let me know if any of you can work extra shifts. I'll add you to the schedule in the computer."

***

Allison woke up at 2:30 p.m., and though she hadn't slept long, she felt energized. She made a cup of coffee, picked up Sean's cell phone and laptop, and found a comfortable spot on the couch to work. She could wait no longer to begin investigating what messages Sean might have left for her.

Other than the unfinished email Detective Derning had shared with her, she found nothing else of interest. But he had told her there was other information she'd find interesting related to hacking the hospital computers.

Where would that be? It must be on his computer. Just as she'd found with his cell phone, she was able to get into the computer without logging on. *Thank you, Detective Derning.* It took her a few minutes to familiarize herself with his computer, but she was able to locate the latest text documents he had saved.

Grateful that he was such an organized person, Allison found four folders, one dated the day of the accident and three from the days leading up to it. She started at the beginning, with a folder titled A.M. Inside the folder were files titled Hospital, SICU Nurses, Schedule, Doctor, and Administration. "This has to be about Andy Marchman," she said, her excitement building.

Opening the file titled SICU Nurses, Allison froze. Inside was a document listing the names of every single SICU nurse, along with personal information for each. This included social security number, date of birth, driver's license number, employee badge number, employment start date, and shift assignment. Some even had personal descriptions noted below their names.

Next to her name was an asterisk, along with the make and model of her car and a reference to her registration information for the hospital parking garage. The same with

Paula Fisher. Sean must have copied this information straight from Marchman's hospital account after he hacked into it.

There was nothing of interest in the Hospital file. Mainly there were JPEG files depicting the layout of various floors and departments in the hospital.

In the file titled Schedule, Allison found monthly schedules for SICU, including both the day and night shifts. The dates went back for a year.

In the folder titled Doctor, there were five subfolders, all relating to only one person, Dr. Joseph Connolly. She remembered Sean's warning about Marchman's possible connection to Joe's murder. Allison paused for a moment, uncertain if she was ready to read what might be in the files. Repositioning herself on the couch and closing her eyes for a few seconds, she took a deep breath and began to explore.

There were five files titled, JC1, JC2, JC3, JC4, and JC5. She opened JC1. She was right. It began with Joe's name and included a lot of personal information likely gleaned from his personnel file at the hospital. The information was public record related to his credentials as a surgeon and privileges at Orlando Memorial Medical Center.

The second folder included information about his car, the Porsche 911, his driver's license number, and his assigned parking spot in the hospital garage. In addition, a series of times reflected Joe's arrival and departure for the six months before his death. *This guy was an animal. He was stalking Joe for six months.*

Now her stomach cramped and her mouth was dry. She took a sip of her coffee, only to discover that it was cold, and then went into the kitchen for some saltines and ice water.

A wave of nausea came over her as her thoughts transported her back to that fateful evening when she had been so happy preparing the romantic dinner for Joe. Tears filled her eyes as she allowed herself to embrace the deep sense of sadness she had pushed away for months. The recent loss of two people she loved was almost more than she could bear.

She pushed the laptop away and stared out the window as a hollow, heavy emptiness settled over her. Other than a friend from her job, she really had no one.

Maybe I'm meant to be alone, to be unhappy. I never did anything to deserve happiness, so why should I expect it? Maybe cynics like Paula are right. "Have no expectations and you're never disappointed." How many times have I heard those words come out of her mouth?

She finished the crackers and water, and her cramping subsided. Wiping her eyes, she decided she had to finish what she'd started.

The file marked JC3 included a list of all of Dr. Connolly's scheduled surgeries and the patient names and dates to coincide. The list went back two years. As Allison scrolled down, she found two names that had been highlighted. One was Peter Wetherly, the SICU patient who had coded and died, and the other was Helen Blanking, Marchman's mother.

In file JC4, Allison found extensive notes related to Wetherly and Blanking and the complications following their surgeries. In the case of Peter Wetherly, she was alarmed to find her name near the end, with dates and times of computer logins. As she scrolled down further, she saw Paula Fisher's name too, with similar notations. The dates coincided with the time he coded and died in SICU. She'd never forget that date. *No wonder Sean warned me about this creep.* When she thought about Marchman, she was glad he was dead.

The last file, JC5, was different from the others. This file did not contain data copied and pasted by Sean from Marchman's computer. Rather it included information Sean had collected himself during his personal investigation of Marchman. Dates included only the days that Sean had been in Florida.

The notes were somewhat cryptic, consisting of phrases. Words like *sociopath* and *revenge* popped up. A summary of Marchman's possible motives was included. Allison read further. "A.M. angry at J.C. for mother's botched surgery. Wanted justice. Believed J.C. got off easy." Then Allison's eyes widened as she read what came next on the screen.

"Google search for gun sales sites in Orlando. Email receipt for .38 pistol and bullets." The date was a week before Connolly was murdered. Allison's fingers froze on the keyboard as the meaning of the words struck home. *Sean had uncovered the motive along with the purchase of a weapon to commit murder. Had Detective Derning seen this? Surely he had. God help us.*

How Allison wished Sean could be here right now so she could discuss these findings with him. Instead, all she had were his words, left for her to find. And now Joe, Marchman, and Sean were all dead, leaving Allison alone with this information and her thoughts.

Overcome by her feelings, she almost missed the final bit of information Sean had documented. "A.M. related to Bobbi Herschfelt. Father?"

How had Sean uncovered all this in only a couple days? If Marchman and Bobbi were related, so many things make sense.

Allison had to find out more, but that was the end of Sean's notes. She searched the rest of the computer but found no other files related to Marchman. How could she discover the nature of the relationship between Marchman and Bobbi? *Could they be siblings? Maybe there is a story as to why Bobbi protected him.* She wondered if Paula knew.

Chapter 39

Bobbi drove home in a daze, arriving at her house as if her car had been on autopilot. It was twelve thirty in the afternoon on a weekday, and she couldn't remember the last time she was at home in the middle of the day. It felt weird. Most people would be glad to be away from work, to have some free time. Bobbi possessed this tremendous sense of guilt and failure. The only reason she was home was because she was forced to resign. Who was she kidding? She'd been fired and the feeling was far from pleasant. She was used to ruling the roost, and now she was down in the dirt and alone.

She didn't even feel like drinking. All sorts of mental images swirled in her mind as she tried to make sense of what had just happened. *How could they have fired me? I have been bending over backward for that place for years. Nobody appreciated all the times I put myself on the line for them.*

Her mind wandered back to the day she accepted the job as director of critical care. Linda Steeling was thrilled to have her, and so were the other administrators. She thought she was hot shit, and she was. When she snapped her fingers, people jumped. She loved the authority and the power that came with the title.

When she realized Paula Fisher, her one-time lover, was a nurse in her unit, she was initially caught off guard but managed to handle the situation, believing she had the upper hand as Paula's direct supervisor.

She became aware of Andy Marchman, but she rarely had to interact with him. Their familial relationship was distant, and she was happy to keep it that way. When he became abusive to her staff after his mother died in her unit, she feared their history could become a problem. But she kept him at bay and made sure she did everything she could to protect him, even at the expense of alienating some of her nurses. He was, after all, her half-brother, and their dark past couldn't be erased. She owed him.

When her nurses came to her about Andy hacking into the computers and threatening them, she let it slide, again using her title to protect him. Even when he made her life difficult with phony emails at work, she couldn't help herself.

Who could have predicted that he'd be charged with the murder of one of their surgeons? Or that he'd end up as a patient in her unit following a heart attack? She'd encouraged her staff to treat him like any other patient.

When he committed suicide in her stepdown unit, she even gave the nurse involved a pass. Anyone looking at the situation objectively would conclude that she had failed, that something wasn't right.

So she knew deep down in her heart that she had been fired for good reason. She had so many mixed feelings. It was too overwhelming to think about everything that had led up to this. She was so physically fatigued that she didn't want to move a muscle. *Maybe a glass of wine would help,* she thought as she trudged to the kitchen. She headed back to the living room, wine glass and bottle in hand, and plopped down on the couch. She poured herself a glass and stared into space as she drank. She yearned for the buzz which would deaden the anguish and erase the hurt. After an hour and a half, the bottle was dry. Feeling no pain, she passed out on her couch.

***

Paula's phone rang. "Hi, Allison. What's up?"

"Nothing. I'm off for a few days. Are you working?" Allison asked.

"No, I'm off tonight and tomorrow. What time is it?"

"It's five thirty. I need to talk to you. Do you want to grab a beer and a bite to eat a little later?"

"Sure. I need at least an hour or so. How about The Whiskey on Sand Lake Road around seven?"

"Okay. That sounds good. I hear their food is good too. I'll meet you there."

Allison was happy for the chance to ask Paula about Bobbi's background, in a place away from the stresses of the hospital. The Whiskey was only a ten-minute drive from her condo, so Allison had some time before she needed to get ready. Closing her eyes, she allowed her mind to wander back to that day in SICU when she realized it might have been Paula who had shut off the alarms the day Mr. Wetherly coded. She hadn't been too impressed with Paula's attitude and questionable integrity then. *Funny how things change. Everyone makes mistakes now and then.* She had come to realize that Paula had a caring side and really was a good nurse. Allison was more determined than ever to expose the corruption that has been covered up for so long at the hospital.

***

Paula had arrived a few minutes early and was seated in a booth in the back of the pub. She waved the server off, telling her she'd wait until her friend arrived. Checking her emails and social media on her phone, the time passed quickly. By 7:10, Paula began to wonder what was keeping Allison. She was never late, and she only lived five minutes away. She decided to send her a text.

"I'm at The Whiskey. It's almost 7:15. Where are you?" Not one to worry without reason, Paula waited a few minutes for a reply. Nothing.

"Hey, girlfriend. Waiting for you at the pub. You ok?" she texted again.

Again, no reply, so Paula called Allison's number. The phone rang five times and then went to voice mail. Paula left a short message.

Paula was just about ready to leave the bar and drive over to Allison's condo when she received the text she'd been waiting for. "I'm ok. Sorry I'm late. Will explain later. Be there in five."

When Allison finally arrived, Paula was relieved.

"I ordered you a beer," Paula said as her friend slid into the seat across from her. "Cheers! To a hell of a week."

Allison raised her glass. "Amen to that!"

"This is good beer. I'm glad we came here. Okay, so tell me the whole story. What was the delay? I'm so glad you're okay."

"You and me both. I was so frustrated that I couldn't communicate with you. You know me; I'm not one to be late."

"I know, so tell me," Paula said.

"Okay. I was all ready to go, practically out the door, and I got a phone call from California. It was from Sean's cousin, who I never met and really don't know. I didn't feel like I could ask her to call back."

"So what did she want?"

Allison took a swig of her beer and her demeanor changed. "Oh, yeah. I was surprised to get that phone call. Her name is Mary Ann."

"So what did she say?"

"She wanted to thank me for everything I did for Sean, although I didn't really do anything. He came out here to help me and ended up dead." Allison paused to hold back the tears.

"She was really nice. She said Sean had never remarried, and she was his closest relative. I guess his parents died years ago, and he had no siblings or children. She informed me he had a life insurance policy from Oracle, his place of employment out there in Silicon Valley, where he moved after we got divorced. Apparently he'd added me to the policy as a contingent beneficiary. She asked for my email and home address for the insurance company so they can contact me to send me the death benefit check. I have no idea how she got my phone number, unless Detective Derning was involved. He told me they'd found some family when they were making arrangements with the funeral home after the investigation. I didn't want to give her my information, even though she seemed genuine and knew enough about Sean. I told her I'd call her back with it. I just wanted to be sure it was the right thing to do."

"She sounds legitimate. But I don't blame you for taking extra precautions. I'm sure she understood. But getting that check would be a nice ending to a terrible situation," Paula said.

"Yeah, but I'd rather have Sean alive any day," Allison said. "Money isn't everything. I never expected to inherit anything from Sean though. Guess I'll believe it when I see it. In the meantime, do you want to get going on the cover-up exposé we've been talking about?"

"Yeah, I do. I'm listening."

"Great! But first I have a question to ask you."

"Go ahead. What do you want to know?"

"When you were with Bobbi, did she ever mention her childhood or her family?"

"Not a lot, but yeah, she did mention them a few times. I don't think she had a good relationship with any of her family members. Why the interest?"

"Well, I was reading some notes Sean made on his laptop. You know he had been investigating the situation at the hospital, and he made some notes about Joe, Marchman, and anything he could tie together. By the way, did you know Marchman had a complete dossier on the SICU nurses? You and I were asterisked with even more info."

"You're kidding," Paula bellowed. "That lousy son of a bitch. I'm glad he killed himself. He did the world a favor."

"I know. I'm glad he's gone too. But anyway, the reason I'm asking about Bobbi's family is that Sean mentioned a possible familial connection between her and Marchman."

"A relationship?" Paula said, wide-eyed. "What kind?"

"I'm not sure. He mentioned Bobbi being related to A.M. and included the word *father*."

"A.M referring to Marchman, I assume."

"I think so," Allison said. "So, can you recall Bobbi ever mentioning a brother or her father?"

"She rarely talked about the past. Let me think back. We're talking years ago."

"I know. Take your time."

"One time when she was pretty drunk she talked about a bad time growing up. She told me she lived on a farm for a while when she was a toddler. Yes, now I remember better. She didn't know the whole story at the time, but she spent a summer at a farm with a family. I seem to recall something about a domineering father and an abusive situation. The man would get drunk and beat up his wife, and Bobbi was afraid."

"Did she say anything else?"

"Yes. I remember because the entire story was so bizarre that I almost didn't believe her. Later I realized it was true. There was a much-older boy who also got beaten by his father. Bobbi later learned this man was her biological father, and she believed that the boy, who would have been her half-brother, protected her from their dad's rage and took the beatings himself."

"How sad. Did she ever mention this brother's name?"

"Not that I can recall. But there was more. Bobbi only mentioned it to me one time, like it was a secret she'd harbored. It seems the brother, who was only a kid himself, ended up retaliating against the father one time, when he was hitting the mother with a belt. He thought the guy was going to kill her if he didn't do something, so he hit him with a baseball bat, and I think he ended up dead."

"Oh my God! Was Bobbi a witness?"

"Yes, she was hiding in the corner, but she saw it. And when it was over, the boy and his mother somehow got rid of the father's body."

Allison was mortified to think her boss had been so traumatized as a child. Her own mother had died when she was a teenager, but the situation was nothing like this.

"How did they do that?"

"If she knew more, she didn't tell me and never mentioned it again. I haven't thought about that conversation for a long time, but it was pretty weird. Maybe they buried his body on the farm. Who would ever know?"

"Wow! It's terrible that a kid would have to kill his father to defend his mother and sister. Do you know what happened to the family after that?"

"I think the mother and son stayed together until he grew up, and Bobbi never went back to the farm after that. Her own parents, her mother and stepfather, were super strict and never knew about any of this."

"Did she ever have any contact with her brother or his mother after that?"

"I don't think so, but I really don't know. She never talked about it. Whenever she did mention family, it was always related to her life in Florida, nothing about a farm except for that one instance. She was young when she moved, so basically her childhood and young adult years here is what she considers home."

"It's probably for the best," Allison said.

"Are you thinking this brother could have been Marchman?" Paula asked.

"It's possible. And it would explain a lot of things, like why Marchman turned out the way he did—antisocial, bitter, evil. And if he'd killed before, he was capable of killing again."

"It would explain why he went so ballistic when his mother died after surgery."

"And why Bobbi acted so weird most of the time. Too bad we'll never know for sure," Allison said.

They focused on their meals, eating in silence as the gravity of the situation threatened to weigh them down. Paula was the first to speak. "Serious stuff, huh? Maybe we should change the subject."

"Yes, let's do it. I was wondering if you thought we could get Tracy on board with our project. She knows a lot that's happened during the day, and between the three of us we should be able to compile a shitload of corrupt practices to expose."

"Do you really think she'd be open to the idea?" Allison wasn't convinced.

"I do. She's smart and on the ball and really isn't a company person. She just knows how to play their game and has been doing it for a long time."

"Okay. Let's contact her soon. In the meantime, let's order another beer and make our list."

Paula flagged down their server and pulled up the notes on her phone. "Here we go. Ready for this?"

Allison nodded. "I'm listening."

Chapter 40

Allison woke up refreshed after the evening with Paula. She could hardly remember the last time she'd enjoyed an evening out in the past year.

After a good night's sleep, her mind was sharp and she was organized and focused. She called Detective Derning but got no answer. She left a brief message and asked him to call her back when he had time. It didn't take long.

"Hi, Allison. Detective Derning. I was on another call. What can I do for you?"

"Good morning, Detective. I have a quick question. I received a call yesterday from Mary Ann Mallory. She told me she was Sean's cousin in California."

"Yes, Allison, she's the one I got in touch with after Sean died."

"Okay. I wanted to ask your opinion about something she said. She told me she was the only family Sean had, and that he had named me as a beneficiary on a life insurance policy he had from work. It dates back to right after our divorce, and he never changed it. From what I understood, there's quite a bit of money involved."

"Go on."

"She asked for my email and home address to give to the insurance company. I hesitated and wanted to double check things with you. I hope I wasn't being stupid. I was wondering how she got my phone number. Did you give it to her, by chance?"

"Ah yes, Allison. I must have forgotten to mention it. I did give her your phone number. I hope you don't mind."

"No, it's fine. I just wanted to be sure everything was on the up and up. I feel relieved now after talking with you. You know my trust in people has been compromised lately. So, you think it's okay if I call her back and give her my information for the insurance company then?"

"Sure, it's fine. We already checked her out. Everything else going as well as can be expected?"

"Yes, it is. I'm trying to resume some sort of normalcy. I even went out with a friend last night."

"Good for you, Allison. Thanks for getting in touch, and don't be a stranger. I'm here if you need anything at all."

"Thanks, Detective. Bye."

Allison was reassured after her conversation with the detective and called Mary Ann back to relay the information. She had to leave a message but would have preferred to speak with her directly to provide her personal addresses.

I guess I'll call Tracy next. Might as well get this ball rolling. She looked at her SICU schedule and placed the call. "Hi, Tracy. It's Allison. Sorry to bother you on your day off. This isn't about work, but it's important."

"No problem, Allison. But first, how are you?"

"I'm okay. Thanks for asking. What I wanted to talk to you about isn't really about work, but it relates to it, in a way. Paula Fisher and I are collaborating on a secret project and would like to include you. Would you be interested in meeting with us to talk about it?"

"Sure, Allison. You've definitely got my curiosity now. What's this about?"

"It's something where we can make a difference, but not in the conventional way. I can tell you more when we meet."

"I'm dying to know more. When did you want to get together?"

"How about lunch one day? I see from the schedule that you're not working tomorrow. Would that be convenient? Paula and I are both off tonight so that would be good for us."

"That's great, Allison. Are you thinking of somewhere in particular?"

"We can meet at Panera Bread, the one near the hospital, if that's good with you. How about 12:30 tomorrow?"

"Okay, Allison. Looking forward to seeing you then."

Allison smiled in anticipation as she ended the call. She allowed herself the luxury of imagining what could be the most successful outcome of her carefully devised strategy. At the same time, a bit of anxiety crept in, just enough to keep her emotions in check. But she knew she was moving forward now and had no intention of looking back.

Chapter 41

Paula replied to Allison's text about lunch at Panera with a short, "Yes. I'll be there."

When Allison arrived at the restaurant, Tracy and Paula were already waiting. The lunch crowd was there, so they got in line to order and then Paula went to find a table.

"I'm addicted to their sandwiches and their soups, especially the turkey and avocado BLT," Allison said as they sat down to eat.

"Yeah, Panera is always a good choice," Tracy said. "They have a big selection and a lot of healthy options. I like the onion soup."

Allison wasted no time getting down to business. "Tracy, we asked you here because we're putting together an exposé, if you will, of the corruption lurking beneath the surface at Orlando Memorial Medical Center. I know you're a charge nurse, but I also know you don't buy everything they feed us, and I'm betting you're disgusted with a lot of their practices."

"It's true. Many times, I've wanted to chuck it all, but I need my job and don't have an alternative at the moment."

"Well, we sort of figured that. What if we kept your name out of it? Paula and I are willing to go out on a limb, maybe even have to quit our jobs and do something else. We don't expect anyone else to be so committed."

"Allison is right, Tracy. We know you have a family, and your job and position are important. We're collecting information ourselves, and we feel you could help by providing us with some of the stuff you know more about. Things that have occurred during the day or management practices you've been privy to. We wouldn't do anything that would jeopardize your position."

"Okay. I'm definitely interested. What kinds of things are you talking about?"

"Are you ready for this?" Paula pulled out the list she'd been compiling and rattled off a string of inefficiencies, unethical occurrences, and unfair practices she'd observed over the past few years at Orlando Memorial Medical Center.

Allison added her own collection of poor practices and underhanded situations she had observed as well. "We're just getting started. The plan is to compile a wealth of information and expose it publicly in various ways."

Paula continued. "We already know it's a big waste of time to report anything through the ethics hotline, because we've already tried it. We thought about news outlets like local TV and even the cable news networks. Maybe even write a book, although that process could take too long. We want something to happen soon."

Allison picked up where Paula left off. "My thought is to use social media. We would create an account on Twitter. Facebook makes you use your own name. The cool thing about Twitter is that it has a wide reach and it's instantaneous. Just think about how Donald Trump used it

Critical Cover-Up

in his political rise to power during the recent political campaign."

"We could tweet every few hours and expose a different corrupt practice or cover-up. The hospital would go nuts. Their PR department isn't big enough to handle the immediate need to respond. The news would certainly get wind of it, because we could tweet it directly to them. Plus, we'd direct the information toward the hospital Twitter account too."

"Do they even have a Twitter account?" Paula asked.

"Yes, I already checked. They are @OrlMemMC. They're not too active, but I guarantee that after this they will be," Allison said with a smile. "Hey, maybe I could offer to manage it for them after this is all out there." She laughed.

A grin snaked across Tracy's face. "This is brilliant. I am definitely in. And if you set up the account and give me access, I can tweet too, because I'm already familiar with Twitter. I learned it because my kids use it. I like to keep track of what they're up to."

"That's great that both of you are familiar with social media," Paula said. "I'm still somewhat old-school, but I can certainly provide the info."

"And with Twitter," Allison interjected, "you only have 140 characters to say something, so it doesn't take long to come up with a short phrase that gets your message across. And we'd also use a hashtag that would hopefully get picked up, something like #CriticalCoverUp."

"I love it," exclaimed Tracy and Paula in unison."

The enthusiasm at lunch had escalated, and the three nurses believed they were on the edge of making a real difference.

"Here, this might be an example of what we'd tweet," Allison said. "Unsafe practices exposed @OrlMemMC. Short staffing forcing SICU RNs to take shortcuts while administration pockets bonuses #CriticalCoverUp."

"Wow! That will get their attention," Tracy said with a grin.

"Or a shorter tweet will allow us to target the news agencies. Here's an example: "Doctors wait weeks for paychecks @OrlMemMC #CriticalCoverUp @CNN @abcnews @cbsnews @nbcnews.

"So we need to compile a list of the issues and then create the tweets so we have enough to keep posting without having to repeat often. The goal is to draw attention to the corrupt practices at the hospital and keep the spotlight on them."

"How long do you think it will take to get this launched?" Tracy asked.

Paula and Allison looked at each other. "You've got my list, Allison, and I can keep coming up with more stuff. You've got about twenty things right there," Paula said.

"It should only take a week or so, I think. My list is that long too. Tracy, do you think you can come up with at least ten issues? Then we'd have fifty problems to talk about. But the important thing to keep in mind is that they have to be real, not made up or embellished. We have to be able to show proof, because at some point, and hopefully soon, the media will want to interview us as part of their investigative reporting. So we want all our ducks in a row."

"Allison, I can think of one right now that you don't even know about. And I can surely come up with nine more. I can have a list for you by tomorrow."

"Fantastic, Tracy. What were you about to tell me? I'm curious."

"I'm interested too," Paula said.

"Well, after Bobbi got fired, they only let her back in her office for a short time. She left a lot of stuff. I had to go in there and clean it out. You won't believe this, but I found a stash of liquor bottles in the back of a filing cabinet drawer. There had to be a dozen of those little bottles like you get on airplanes. Only a few were unopened. The rest were either empty or half empty."

"Oh my God, you're kidding me. She was drinking at work?" Allison asked,

"Not sure, but she could have been. Maybe when she was in her office before she left for home. Who knows? I never smelled alcohol on her breath."

"Wow! She had a bigger problem than we ever knew."

Tracy continued. "And that wasn't all. On her desk, beneath some books, I found stacks of applications that had never been reviewed."

"You mean applications from nurses?"

"Yeah, applying for full-time positions in SICU. She never reviewed them, and we were always short-staffed until the hospital hired travelers. We could have had full-time nurses."

"That is unacceptable," Allison exclaimed. "That's definitely getting tweeted out."

"I think once you start with your list, the easier it's going to be to come up with more instances of corruption and unethical practices," Paula said.

"I'm excited," said Allison. "I think I've got more than enough to get started."

"And I may reconsider my need to be in the background on this. This may become too big, and I might want to be more involved," Tracy said.

"Okay, Tracy. But for now you'll stay incognito. Just let Paula and me know if and when the time comes."

The three finished their meals and all acknowledged with shared exuberance that they'd had a productive meeting. Allison couldn't wait to get home to begin writing.

Chapter 42

When Bobbi awoke it was already dark. *Where am I? What time is it?* She grabbed her phone and squinted at the screen. 9:30 p.m. She hadn't eaten and had no appetite. All she wanted to do was forget about everything. She noticed the empty Pinot Grigio bottle on the coffee table.

She trudged to the kitchen and opened another bottle. *Why, God, have you forsaken me? Please let me just go to sleep so I don't have to think about any of this.* All she wanted was for this day to end and for everything to be okay. She stumbled back to the couch in a daze and kept drinking until she couldn't remember anything else.

The following day Bobbi awoke to sunlight streaming through the windows. It was three o'clock in the afternoon. She looked down to find herself still dressed in the work clothes she'd worn the day before, disgusted by the flecks of dried vomitus scattered across the top.

Two empty wine bottles stood on the coffee table. The constant dull ache in the front of her head forced her to confront reality. For many years she'd tried to deny it, but she knew she was a drunk, just like her biological father had been. She despised herself.

Isolated and overwhelmed, she somehow managed to get to the bathroom. Her mouth felt like sandpaper and her breath smelled foul. She took a long hot shower and washed her hair. She stood in there a long time, as if she needed the same amount of time she spent on her drunken binge to wash off the consequences of it. After she dried off, brushed her teeth, and wrapped her head in a towel, she threw on a pair of yoga pants and a T-shirt. She made coffee and drank two glasses of water. Still not hungry, numb and cold, she was alone. Bobbi picked up her phone and called the only person who came to mind.

***

Paula never expected to see Bobbi's name on the caller ID. Hesitating only a few seconds, she answered. "Bobbi?"

At first, only silence filled the space between them. Then a different-sounding Bobbi replied. "Paula, thank God you're there. I didn't know who else to call."

After what seemed like endless silence, Paula eventually replied. "I'm here, Bobbi. You sound like something's wrong. I heard you resigned."

"Resigned? Those motherfuckers fired me, forced me to resign, and for no reason. I gave up my whole life for them and for what? This shit? Well, I don't need them."

Bobbi's tone was belligerent, and Paula didn't want to listen to it. She'd heard it before, whenever Bobbi was drunk.

"Bobbi, I know you've been drinking. Do you think I can't tell? You need help, Bobbi. You're an alcoholic and need AA, or you're never going to get past this. You need to report yourself to the Florida Board of Nursing. They can help you with the impaired nurse program or whatever it's called."

"How dare you tell me what I need!" Bobbi shouted into the phone. "You think you know me, but you don't know shit. I don't need you or anyone else. Fuck all of you."

Paula debated between hanging up or continuing to talk with Bobbi. She decided on the latter but not in a sympathetic way. Instead, she confronted her with the hard truth and gave her an option.

"Bobbi, you're angry and you aren't making any sense. The hospital had every reason to fire you. You allowed a lot to go on during your watch, and you got caught. There's more coming too. I've heard stuff. Bobbi, I'm telling you honestly, the only option for you is to get yourself to AA."

Bobbi wasn't having any of it. "You don't know what you're talking about. I don't need AA, and I certainly don't need you telling me what to do. Shove it up your ass. I never should have called you."

***

Paula wasn't too surprised when Bobbi abruptly ended the call. It was sad to watch an ex-lover spiral downward into such a deep hole. She doubted Bobbi'd get out without a desire to do so, and at this point, that aspiration was nonexistent. Paula would continue to help Allison and Tracy expose as much cover-up and corruption in the hospital as possible, and that did not exclude Bobbi.

Chapter 43

Linda was meeting with Tracy, the SICU charge nurse, when the text from the ER came through.

"Damn. I've got to go. Good to talk to you, Tracy," she said before hurrying downstairs. She approached the reception desk in the ER and leaned in close. "I got a text that Bobbi Herschfelt just came in as an OD. Where is she?"

The unit secretary directed her toward the closest bay. The ER doctor and a nurse were at the bedside, directing the scene. Bobbi had already been intubated and was on the ventilator. Her monitor showed a normal heart rhythm and blood pressure. "How is she?"

"She's been unresponsive since they found her, and she has no spontaneous respirations. We've got her on pressors. We're waiting on the drug screen."

"Okay. Keep me posted, please. Is there any family?"

"None that we know of at this point."

"I think there was an ex-husband. We'll have someone look into it," Linda said. Before she left the ER, she directed the nursing supervisor to locate the next of kin. "Also, find a bed for her in MICU, even if it means making

Critical Cover-Up

a lateral transfer. I don't want her going to SICU. They've had enough to deal with recently." Despite the fact that Bobbi had been the director of both critical care units, SICU was larger and busier, and the main unit out of which she operated. Linda was thinking worst-case scenario—that Bobbi might be there for a while and never wake up.

In normal circumstances, staff nurses took care of their own. If a nurse or member of their family required admission to an ICU, they preferred to have that person in their unit and took special care to assign them the best nurses. VIP treatment for one of their own. In this instance, Bobbi was not well-liked by the staff, so nobody spoke up to request to have her in SICU.

On the way back to her office, Linda called Tracy to tell her the news. "I apologize for leaving our meeting so abruptly," she said. "I wanted you to hear this from me. Bobbi just came in through the ER, unresponsive and on a vent. I'm admitting her to MICU. I thought your nurses could use a reprieve."

"What happened?" Tracy asked, stunned and genuinely concerned.

"Overdose. We think it's opiates and benzos, but they don't have the drug screen results yet. Is everything good there?"

"We're managing. We're short a nurse, because one of the travelers didn't show."

"I'm telling you, we got a bad batch of travelers this time. Just do the best you can. And thank you for all that you do every day."

Linda hung up the phone, content with herself for managing her job so efficiently. On the other end of the line, Tracy rolled her eyes, unimpressed by Linda's phony concern.

***

Allison stayed up half the night writing tweets for their Critical Cover-Up project. She was on a roll, motivated like she'd been when she first transferred to SICU. It seemed odd that although it wasn't that long ago, her life had changed so much.

I can't wait to share these with Paula tonight at work. And when I get Tracy's list, I'll have even more material. To say she was psyched would be an understatement. She was hoping to have at least fifty tweets done by that night. So far she had completed twenty:

> Hospital doctors wait weeks for paychecks @OrlMemMC #CriticalCoverUp @CNN @abcnews @cbsnews @nbcnews
>
> Unsafe practices exposed @OrlMemMC Short staffing forcing SICU RNs to take shortcuts while administrators pocket bonuses #CriticalCoverUp #Unsafe
>
> RNs @OrlMemMC told to clock out for lunch even if they don't have time to take a lunch #UnfairLaborPractices #Fraud #CriticalCoverUp

And that was only the beginning. The other tweets were just as powerful, and all contained reference to the #CriticalCoverUp project and a slew of hashtags. No department was immune to the attack.

Hospital shortages create unhealthy work environment @OrlMemMC.
Nurses @OrlMemMC working constant overtime to point of exhaustion @FlNursingBoard.

Alcohol found @OrlMemMC in desk of critical care director @orlandosentinel #addictednurses.

Your taxes pay for security guards to sit 24/7 with comatose patient @OrlMemMC #Governmentwaste.

The tweets continue with:

Doctors' pay @OrlMemMC based on how many procedures they do, not on skill or expertise.

Surgeon murdered in parking garage of @OrlMemMC and surveillance camera said to be inactive.

Hospital Information Security Senior Engineer hacks into staff emails @OrlMemMC.

Travel nurse @OrlMemMC caught stealing narcotics #Drugdiversion.

Critical alarms turned off @OrlMemMC #PatientSafety #AlarmFatigue.

Inefficient mandatory duplicate electronic and paper charting @OrlMemMC increases workload for nursing staff.

Patient hangs himself in bathroom @OrlMemMC while security guard sleeps.

And more tweets:

Nurses forced to work short @OrlMemMC so hospital board member can have 1:1 attention @CNN @abcnews #UnfairLaborPratice.

Overtime paid to nurses who stay late to document due to 3-patient assignments in ICU @OrlMemMC #Heavyworkload @NLRB.

Critical care RNs ordered to empty trash and linens so @OrlMemMC can eliminate housekeeping staff to save money #Moneybottomline.

Doctor denies performing unnecessary procedures in cath lab to increase revenue for @OrlMemMC @CNN @AMA.

Hospital admits patients to ICU without meeting criteria to lower ER wait times @OrlMemMC #unethical @CNN.

Nurse manager @OrlMemMC smuggles liquor into hospital on New Year's Eve and orders staff to deny.

Hospital destaffs RNs to save labor cost and forces them to be on call without pay #Unfairlaborpractices@OrlMemMC@NLRB.

Allison looked at her list of tweets and felt a sense of accomplishment. *That didn't take long, and I know I can easily come up with more. I can't wait to see what Paula and Tracy have on their lists.* For the first time in a quite a while she looked forward to going to work again.

Chapter 44

It had been four days since Bobbi Herschfelt was admitted to MICU. Her condition had worsened. She remained vented and never showed any signs of waking up. Her EEG showed diffuse activity, and she was fully dependent on the ventilator with no spontaneous respirations. Her kidneys were shutting down, and the medical staff had been discussing options with her ex-husband, who was her next of kin and legal health care surrogate.

In light of their strained relationship, he no longer felt any emotional tie to her. He had remarried and moved on and was only there because he had to be. The sad truth was, there was nobody else.

He wasn't comfortable with making a decision to take her off the vent, especially since she had some brain activity. But he also didn't want to give permission for any life-extending procedures such as dialysis. The decision was made to send Bobbi to a long-term care facility, one that specialized in taking care of vented patients. He knew she would eventually die there, and he wouldn't have to concern himself with her any longer. The one tie he still had to Bobbi was this lack of compassion and feeling.

Maybe he learned it from her. He didn't know and didn't care.

***

At 4:30 that afternoon, Linda Steeling watched in silence as Bobbi was loaded into the transport ambulance and transferred to the other facility. Most of the nurses in MICU were travelers and had no real connection to Bobbi. None of her former staff in SICU even knew that the person who, until recently, had wielded such authority over them had departed the hospital in such an anonymous way.

***

Paula was home and had completed her list to share with Allison. This entire process had triggered some introspection and prompted her to contemplate her future. Having worked in hospitals for many years, she realized that their cover-up project would expose her hospital to public scrutiny and investigation. As soon as their roles became public knowledge, their jobs would certainly be jeopardized. Orlando Memorial Medical Center had a reputation for firing nurses for reasons far less than this.

She remembered the shock she'd felt the day one of the best nurses in the unit had been fired. Mark was a charge nurse with a reputation as a highly skilled and experienced critical care nurse. He had been called "a walking encyclopedia of knowledge." Not only was he one of the best resources, but he had a great sense of humor, was well-liked, and was fun to work with. He could carry on a conversation with anyone.

Margie Miklas

Paula smiled as she recalled how he'd start a casual dialogue with his patient. "So where are you from?" More often than not, no matter which city or town was named, Mark would continue with, "Oh, I had an uncle from there. He had a furniture company." Or "Oh, I used to go fishing there." And these were real facts. Uncanny.

Mark was passionate in what he believed, and he was assertive when he needed to be. One day he stood up to the nursing administration for something he believed was right, refusing to accept a patient who was infected. In an ideal situation, infected patients shouldn't be admitted to a surgical ICU with fresh post-op patients. His actions generated a phone call from the CNO. In front of everyone in the unit, he did the unthinkable and yelled "Fuck you" into the phone before slamming it down. That was the last day he worked at Orlando Memorial Medical Center. No discussion, no negotiation. Maybe if there had been a nurses' union things would have ended differently. A topic for another day.

So Paula's thoughts turned to options for herself. She wasn't in a relationship and hadn't been in a long time, actually since her tryst with Bobbi, so she felt free to go wherever she pleased. That was the great thing about having a nursing license. You could go anywhere and work.

Since she and Allison had become such close friends, she wouldn't mind continuing to work together. *Maybe we could apply for a travel assignment together.* She had heard how nice it was in California, with mandated nurse-patient ratios and high salaries. One of her friends was always emailing her about making all this overtime pay and never having more than two patients in ICU. She made a mental note to discuss this option with Allison.

***

Allison slept late since this was a work night for her. While she was eating her breakfast, and giving Snowball some much-needed attention, she caught up on her email and the stack of snail mail she had accumulated. A letter from New York Life Insurance Company grabbed her attention. Upon opening it, she read the cover letter which verified that she was the beneficiary of a death benefit for Sean McNally. She continued reading. "You will find all the necessary forms required to file the claim. Please include a copy of the death certificate." She recalled having seen an email about this a week ago but had forgotten about it. *The death certificate. Where would it be? The coroner? Orange County Health Department?* She vaguely remembered a patient's family member mentioning that he had picked one up at the Vital Statistics Department on Church Street and that they cost about ten dollars.

It's only about a twenty-minute drive from here. I might as well get this out of the way. Allison got dressed and drove to the location, remembering to bring cash and the insurance company letter with her.

By some sheer force of luck, she only had to wait fifteen minutes and was on her way back home with the required official documentation in less than an hour. She hadn't looked at it except to see that Sean's name was on it.

Once inside her condo, she sat down on the couch to read the death certificate. A minute later, tears blurred her vision and she had to wipe her eyes in order to read the rest of the document. Listed as the immediate cause of death was "hemorrhagic shock secondary to ruptured aorta as a result of motor vehicle crash." Reading the stark words in black and white underscored the reality for Allison that the only love of her life was gone forever. Allison lay down and sobbed.

***

After arriving in the unit that evening, Allison touched base with Paula, who told her she had the list for their project. "Great, I have mine too. We're going to do this."

She checked her assignment, delighted to find Tracy behind the desk. "Hi, Tracy. Did you bring the information?"

"Yes, I'll give it to you after you get report. I'll be here for a while."

"Okay, sounds good." Allison was eager to get started and sought out Connie for report on her patients.

"Hi, I'm a little behind, but I can give you report and finish up afterward."

She was surprised at Connie's comment. This was one of Allison's biggest pet peeves. *Some things never change. She'll be here charting for the next hour, collecting overtime. The hospital continues to reward inefficiency with extra pay, yet sends people home in the middle of a shift to save money. So stupid.* She made a mental note to include this in a tweet.

Her assignment didn't seem too bad, despite the fact that she had three patients. Two had transfer orders, so if they got bed assignments, things could change. She could end up having to transfer them both out plus get two new admissions.

After report, she found Tracy, who handed her the list. "I'm still on the fence about my involvement being made public, Allison. You gave me your word you'd leave my name out of this, right? I still need my job."

"Yes. Don't worry, Tracy. You are a silent partner for now," Allison said.

"Thanks. If I come up with any more thoughts, I'll write them down and get them to you."

"Okay, great. We're planning to go public with this next week," Allison said. "I'll keep you posted." Allison knew she had to concentrate on her patients, but she was psyched. She needed to get the list from Paula tonight too. Her head was full of ideas now that the three of them were collaborating.

Halfway through their shift, Paula spoke with Allison. "I was thinking . . . once this is out and the hospital learns we're involved, you know our jobs are toast. Now is the time to plan ahead. Have you considered the travel nurse option? I'd love to go to California. Everyone I know out there loves it."

"Yeah, I have. I think it's a good option. Do you already have your California license?"

"I do, but you need to apply now, so we'll be ready to go when we have to. I'm still with my travel nurse agency. Maybe you should sign up," Paula said.

"Good thought. I'll do it later when I'm home. We can still work on our project, no matter what state we're in. I've been brainstorming, and this is what I've come up with. Tell me what you think."

Allison and Paula strolled past the patient rooms to the end of the unit where they could talk more discreetly. "This week, maybe later today if I have enough time, I'm going to register the Twitter site, Critical Cover-Up, and our Twitter name will be @CriticalCoverUp. I'll also start a website with the same name. I've already researched it, and no one has that domain. We'll use the hashtag #CriticalCoverUp. Want to hear a few examples of my ideas in action?"

"Sure," Paula said with a smile and even more enthusiasm.

"Okay, here goes:

> Hospital staff @OrlMemMC falsify records to increase Medicare and Medicaid payments #Fraud @CNN #CriticalCoverUp.
>
> Is your hospital committing fraud? We can help. Contact Critical Cover-Up at https://www.CriticalCover-Up.com #Fraud #MedicareFraud.
>
> Attention nurses. Are you experiencing #Patientsafety issues at your hospital? #CriticalCoverUp Notify Critical Cover-Up at https:// CriticalCover-Up.com.

"What do you think?"

"I love it. You're really good at social media," Paula said.

Allison smiled. "Thanks. It's a powerful tool. And you get instantaneous response and engagement. I think we're going to be doing a good thing. And there's no telling where this will go. Maybe national. I'm envisioning other nurses, physicians, and facilities sending us information."

"That would be fantastic. This could become a regular business," Paula said, handing her list to Allison. "Here you go."

"Thanks. I'll let you know when everything is up and running. Text me the link to your travel nurse agency so I can sign up with them too."

"I will. It's Medical Staffing Solutions, but I'll text you the link."

"Thanks, Paula. You know there is a possibility that we can stay incognito for a while, but it's better to have all our ducks in a row. You know what I mean?"

"Yeah, I agree."

Allison finished her shift without having to transfer her patients, because no beds became available. Leaving the hospital, she felt inspired. Ten days ago she'd been a wreck. She could never have anticipated that she might really be able to make an impact in nursing, but in a different sort of way. Now she actually believed it.

Chapter 45

Allison was awake early. After her coffee, she planned to focus on her new project. First things first, though. With the paperwork for the insurance company complete, she mailed the form along with the death certificate.

Next, she checked out the California Board of Nursing website and reviewed the requirements for licensure by endorsement. She noted that the processing time was usually twelve weeks, which would be okay for her. She made a list of what was required before she could file the online application.

She needed to have a passport-size photograph, a verification of her current nursing license from the Florida Board of Nursing, and she'd need to file a fingerprint card after having them taken at a local law enforcement agency. *I can contact Detective Derning for that.* She also had to have certified copies of her transcripts forwarded directly from her nursing school in Florida. Finally, she needed to submit payment of $149.

This entire process could take about four months. She thought she'd be good that long without a job, but she really didn't think she was going to get fired. *They aren't that smart. By the time they figure out who is behind Critical Cover-Up it will be at least a few months.*

Next, she found her resume and updated it, which only took ten minutes. She searched for the travel nurse website Paula had texted her. She located the application and submitted it with resume attached. Simple.

She still had several hours before she had to leave for work, so she established a Twitter site and wrote a blurb describing it: "Uncovering corrupt practices and fraud inside healthcare facilities." She scrolled through a free photo site and selected a generic image—a doctor in scrubs walking out of an emergency room—to use as her profile photo.

Now she needed to post a few tweets to get started. She didn't want to launch anything about Orlando Memorial Medical Center yet, so she posted the following nonspecific tweet: "Attention nurses. Are you experiencing patient safety issues at your hospital? Share your experiences here #CriticalCoverUp."

Since Twitter no longer included images in their 140-character limit, she added an image of healthcare personnel in scrubs. Then she did a search for #nurses and #doctors and followed thirty of their Twitter accounts. She'd post a couple new tweets every day until she was ready to start with the targeted tweets about @OrlMemMC.

In between, she'd post news articles citing recent events and situations across the country where these issues had already been publicized. One of the more recent ones referred to Medicare fraud and physician kickbacks to a large corporate health care company. They had to pay over $500 million in fines and faced charges related to criminal court cases and civil lawsuits.

Margie Miklas

She knew she had to get a website going, so she reviewed the top website builders and registered, selected a template, and started inputting information. Grateful for her computer experience when she worked in real estate, Allison found this work quite simple to do. She left the website in draft mode until she had time to properly complete the setup and add more material and some images. But for now she owned the domain name, criticalcoverup.com. Allison couldn't help feeling pleased.

She still had an hour before she had to go to work, so she reviewed the lists she had received from Paula and Tracy. Both nurses had worked in SICU for several years before Allison transferred there. She could hardly believe some of the things she read.

Tracy's list consisted of only five items, but they were shocking discoveries for Allison, stories she had never heard before now:

> Supervisor leaves hospital to attend birthday party, consumes alcohol, and returns to work, on the clock the entire time. No repercussion. Cozy with CNO.

> Nurse manager brings in supply of liquor for Team A during hurricane. Colludes with staff to hide evidence.

> Cardiologists keep beer cold in cath lab refrigerator and party after emergency cases.

> Nurse manager, drunk, phones SICU in middle of night and directs charge nurse to leave the hospital to pick her up and drive

her home.

> Supervisor floats SICU RN to MICU and replaces with stepdown nurse. Patient safety issues.

Paula's list was not quite as shocking but was, nevertheless, an eye-opener for Allison. Most of the items involved short-staffing and patient safety issues that had occurred before Allison's time in SICU. Also mentioned were bullshit-type situations such as:

> Nurses encouraged to fill out physician disciplinary form but nothing ever happens. Good-old-boy club.

> Favoritism toward nurses who party with unit director outside of work. Drinking buddies.

> Frequent practice of floating a nurse to another unit and sending a nursing assistant to replace. Lame and unsafe.

> Rewards nurses who consistently stay late to chart by paying incidental overtime, yet counsels other nurses who clock in too early with threats of suspension.

Paula didn't mince words. A good start to Allison's current list of corruptive practices and unethical situations. She looked at the clock. It was time to get ready for another shift.

Margie Miklas

***

Since this was such a busy night in the unit, Allison found no time to think about her new scheme. She was assigned to only one patient, who was extremely unstable, having been admitted from PACU a few hours earlier in hemorrhagic shock. John Bradley was young, a passenger in a high-speed motor vehicle crash in which the driver had died. He had suffered multiple injuries, the worst being intra-abdominal trauma and peritonitis as a result of a lacerated liver, ruptured spleen, and perforated colon. She worked hard all night to keep him alive.

It was all she could do to maintain an adequate blood pressure despite multiple transfusions and vasoactive IV drips. By the morning he was still bleeding from somewhere and likely would have to return to surgery. He was a train wreck, but she found the challenge exhilarating. In the back of her mind, she believed she was doing this for Sean, who never had a chance.

When the day shift nurse showed up to get report, Allison was exhausted. Grateful to see her replacement, Allison was stunned to learn that Barbara, a travel nurse, had been assigned a second patient, who was critically ill and ventilated.

"This is impossible. He's still actively bleeding and hemodynamically unstable. I haven't left his side all night. There's no way you'll be able to handle another patient too. Get the charge nurse."

Barbara did as she was told, returning a couple minutes later with Penny, the relief charge nurse who covered for Tracy on her day off.

Critical Cover-Up

"Penny, this assignment isn't feasible," Allison said, explaining the situation. "I've been working almost nonstop all night just trying to keep him alive. He's extremely unstable. There is no way that even the most experienced critical care nurse can handle him plus another patient."

"What's the matter? He's not a fresh post-op anymore. Why would he need to be a 1:1?" While guidelines exist for 1:1 nurse-patient ratios, they are not always clear-cut.

Clearly exasperated by Penny's judgment in making the nursing assignment, Allison stepped just outside her patient's room so he wouldn't hear any of the conversation, despite the fact that he was sedated. "Didn't you hear about him in charge report?" Allison asked, waving her arms and pointing back toward the patient, who was surrounded by multiple IV pumps and lifesaving equipment. "He's still bleeding, and his vitals are all over the place. I've been on the phone with the surgeon throughout the night. He's received six units of packed cells, and I'm barely maintaining a pressure with Levophed."

"Well, we're running one nurse short, and I have no one else. Barbara will have to do the best she can. And I'll be here to help." Penny turned around and walked back to the nurses' station, unfazed.

Allison knew this was completely unsafe. She wished Tracy was in charge today. She'd never let this happen. Allison gave report to Barbara and then called the surgeon to tell him what was going on. He screamed into the phone and asked Allison if she could stay until he arrived. Feeling an obligation, she agreed.

"Can you get here in an hour or less?"

"I'm on my way," he said.

Allison knew nothing would be accomplished by going up the chain of command and calling the CNO, but felt she needed to, just to cover herself. She called the hospital operator and asked to be connected to Linda's cell number. She was surprised when the CNO answered on the second ring.

"Linda, this is Allison Jamison. I'm a night nurse in SICU. There's an urgent issue here affecting patient safety. I'm calling to make you aware of it. I've already spoken with Penny, the charge nurse."

"What is the issue, Allison?"

Allison summarized the situation to Linda, highlighting the crucial concerns. "I'm going off shift, and the nurse taking over my assignment—a critically unstable, bleeding patient—was also assigned another patient on a vent. I'm quite concerned because my patient's deteriorating condition dictates 1:1 nursing care. If you can come up here, I'm sure you will see for yourself the gravity of the situation."

"All right, Allison. I wasn't aware of any staffing issues in your unit this morning. I'll talk to the charge nurse and see what I can do." Allison thanked her before ending the call.

With no real certainty that anything would change, Allison continued to care for John Bradley while Barbara got report on her other patient. Allison felt no need to inform Penny of her decision to contact the surgeon or the CNO.

Ten minutes later, Penny entered Bradley's room and informed Allison that she didn't appreciate her contacting the CNO behind her back. "I'm the charge nurse, and I'm handling the situation here. Apparently, you didn't agree and had to go crying to administration. Now Linda's coming up here. I hope you're satisfied."

Critical Cover-Up

Allison never understood why nurses didn't stand behind each other. Rather than focusing on the right thing to do, many of them tended to eat their young instead. Case in point. Maybe this is what happens as you climb up the ladder. But Tracy wasn't this way.

Allison smiled, glad she'd created a stir. The situation warranted it. *They get all bent out of shape for stupid things like not changing the suction canisters every day or having the date wrong on the IV tubing, yet something of this magnitude, where a patient's life is at stake, didn't seem to mean as much.*

Barbara popped her head into Allison's patient's room to thank her for staying and buying her some time. "I really appreciate this, Allison. You knew I was overwhelmed."

"I understand, Barbara. The surgeon will be in soon, and the CNO is on her way up here to assess the situation. Hopefully the assignment will be changed. Maybe they'll find another nurse somehow."

Allison secretly hoped Linda and the surgeon would arrive at the same time. That way he could unfurl his wrath over his patient's safety onto a hospital administrator instead of the poor nurse. This was exactly the kind of nonsense that needed to be publicized. Most people had no idea that hospitals operated in this manner.

Linda appeared first and asked for a summary of the patient's current status. While Allison titrated his drips and hung another unit of blood, she gave her a quick verbal report. The monitor was in full view, so Linda should have been able to determine that his blood pressure was marginal. "Dr. Mayfair is on his way in now."

"All right. I can clearly see that he needs to stay 1:1. We'll figure a way to get you another nurse, even if I have to short another unit."

Linda walked out of the room and found Penny. "Call the nurse you destaffed and tell him he has to come in. The situation is too unstable in Room 3, and I don't need Dr. Mayfair yelling at me again."

When Allison overheard this conversation, she seethed. The staffing had been adequate, but to save money and look good to the hospital board, nursing administration routinely responded to pressure to destaff nurses and save on labor costs, especially during the last few weeks of the quarter. That's exactly why they were short a nurse today. Utilizing a flexible staffing model, they staff to a minimum based on a calculated daily average census. Patient care suffered and employee satisfaction did too. But the owners of the hospital loved it.

Dr. Mayfair showed up at 8:00 a.m., and after assessing his patient's clinical status and lab reports for less than five minutes, he called the OR to let them know he'd be bringing the patient back for more surgery. Then he turned to Allison. "Order four more units of packed cells, and keep two on hold at all times. Good call, Allison."

Dr. Mayfair found the charge nurse and told her he was taking John Bradley back for bleeding and that he was going to write an order that the patient would stay 1:1 until he cancelled it. He followed up by calling the CNO and reading her the riot act.

"Don't you know what's going on in your own units? My patient bled all night long and is only alive thanks to one of your SICU nurses. Yet this morning you okayed him to be paired with another vented patient? At least when Bobbi was here she knew when a patient needed to be a 1:1 without being told."

Allison overheard the doctor's harsh conversation with Linda, because he was still in the hall near the SICU door.

The corners of her mouth curved upward in the slightest way as she approved of the surgeon's lashing out. She felt a sense of accomplishment and she knew she did the right thing. Yes, she could make a difference.

By 8:45 a.m. she'd reported off to Barbara and walked out of the hospital, exhausted, yet energized.

Chapter 46

"So you're moving to California?" Detective Derning was genuinely surprised when Allison showed up at the station to inquire about getting fingerprinted.

"Well, I haven't decided, but I'm seriously thinking about it. Travel nursing is a good gig, and if you're going to do it, California is the place to go."

"Well, I wish you the best, Allison. You deserve it."

"Thank you, Detective. I appreciate everything you've done for me. I'll never forget it."

"Just doing my job. But if you ever need anything, you know how to get in touch with me."

Allison was grateful to know she had a male friend she could trust. She had completed everything she needed for her California license application, and the fingerprint card was the last piece. On her way home, she mailed the packet to the California Board of Registered Nursing in Sacramento.

Medical Staffing Solutions had contacted her, and she had taken the credentialing tests they required and spoken with a recruiter. Everything had been approved and was on hold until she gave them a date that she'd be available for an assignment in California.

Not long after she arrived back home, her doorbell rang. She could see a UPS delivery guy waiting with a packet. Allison opened the door and he said, "Overnight delivery, Ma'am. I need your signature, please."

She signed her name and thanked him, closing the door. The return address was New York Life Insurance Company. She had almost forgotten about this, but without delay, she opened the packet and pulled out an envelope. She had been curious about the death benefit she was told she'd receive, but never in her wildest dreams could she have anticipated what was inside.

Could this be true? Half a million dollars? Stunned, she found this almost impossible to believe. She had never inherited a dime before now. When her mother died, there wasn't anything to inherit. Allison had lived fairly well when she was a realtor, but she had worked hard for years before she earned a six-figure salary. And even though nursing salaries today are considered lucrative, she wasn't making close to six figures, even with overtime. Only the nurses with at least ten years of experience and much higher base salaries were making over $100K a year, and that's if they worked extra shifts.

This kind of money could provide all sorts of options, especially if she invested it well. Her mind was filled with ideas about possibilities for the future, especially with her cover-up project in the forefront. With a faint smile, she put the letter away and decided to focus on her scheme to expose her hospital's corruptive practices.

She signed onto the internet, more driven than ever toward her goal. Allison had been spending most of her free time on Twitter. She could understand how addicting it was for so many users. In a little less than a week, Allison had become fairly adept at Twitter, interacting with other users and following accounts she thought would be beneficial to her mission. She now had over 300 followers and was getting a lot of retweets and comments. She had learned how to compile lists and create appropriate hashtags.

Now that Allison also had posted enough newsworthy and educational content to her website, she figured it was time to go live with the entire project, both on her website and via Twitter. The process mimicked the satisfaction of starting up a business and felt exciting.

The reaction the first week was better than she had hoped for. Nurses, patients, physicians, and even attorneys across the country, and a few in the UK and Australia, had responded. What she liked about Twitter was that she could access it anywhere she had an internet connection, so her smartphone was perfect for it. Reactions were swift, so it was important to be able to respond and interact in a timely manner. For this reason, she enabled her notifications with sound.

She continued making lists of hashtags she could use, like #healthcarefraud, #whistleblower, #medicarefraud, #understaffed, #staffingratios, #overworkednurses, #patientsafety, #hospitalcorruption, #medicalerrors, and #surgicalscrewups.

The responses she received from health care professionals around the country encouraged Allison. They tweeted about the same problems. If she could expose other health care facilities the way she was doing with her own hospital, maybe she could increase awareness enough to attract the attention of news organizations and consumer groups who actually had some clout.

Lots of nurses' unions and lawyers were engaging with her via Twitter as well. She found it interesting that health care facilities with active Twitter accounts actually replied to targeted complaints, much like the customer service department of a business. Allison had seen tweets from airlines and cable companies doing the same. Whether these tweets could actually effect change wasn't clear though. Twitter sites belonging to hospitals that only tweeted every week or so, like Orlando Memorial Medical Center, wouldn't even notice the posts directed toward them until a week went by.

Allison began posting tweets mentioning negative situations at Orlando Memorial using their Twitter name, @OrlMemMC, and the #criticalcoverup hashtag. Every so often she'd add a news organization's hashtag to it, so that if @OrlMemMC didn't notice the tweet directed toward them, perhaps @NBCNews or the local news stations would see it and investigate. She relished this.

After three hours on the computer, she needed a break and called her friend. "Hi, Paula. How's it going?"

"Not bad. What have you been up to? Let me guess. Working on the computer, right? We've been working opposite each other for the past couple of nights. I wasn't feeling that great, so I slept a lot during the daytime."

"Oh, I'm sorry to hear that. Anything serious?"

"No, just my sinuses. I'm much better today, thanks."

"Well, I'm glad you're better now. Are you in the mood to hear what I've been doing?"

"Sure. Go ahead. I'm all ears."

"Listen, I've been on a roll. You're right, I've been on the computer developing the website and working on social media all week. It's going even better than I expected."

"That's cool. And not a word from the hospital?"

"No, not yet. I just started the tweets directed toward them. We'll see how long it takes for them to get wind of it. I imagine we'll hear about it at work soon, either by email or a staff meeting."

"So where are you with the other stuff—the travel agency and the California license? I updated all my information with my travel nurse agency," Paula said.

"I mailed it all off today. But I'm all set up with Medical Staffing Solutions too."

"Sounds good. Everything is set then."

"I'm really invested in this Critical Cover-Up project, Paula. It feels like I'm starting a business."

"And the good thing is you can do it from anywhere. This doesn't have to be only about this hospital. We both know these corrupt practices go on at other places too."

"You're right about that. I'm already learning about a lot stuff that goes on from the responses I'm getting on Twitter."

"We can talk more about it later. I think Cali would be fun," Paula said. "When do you work again?"

"Tomorrow. I'm on for three nights in a row," Allison said.

"Okay. Tomorrow's my last night for a while, so I'll see you then."

"Sounds good, Paula. Get some rest."

Allison didn't say anything to Paula about the life insurance money, but it was in the back of her mind, as sort of a cushion. It would allow her the opportunity to take a leave from hospital nursing, to focus on her new business or, who knows, maybe write a book, an exposé. The possibilities seemed endless.

Chapter 47

In her cubicle in the back of the Information Security department at Orlando Memorial Medical Center, Terry Hanley settled in to start her work week. It was Monday morning, and a few of the IT guys were already working. She rarely interacted with them, preferring to work alone and in a quiet environment. Her role as public relations assistant seemed like an oxymoron, since she wasn't actually in the public eye, preferring to stay behind the scenes. Luckily her gregarious boss enjoyed the spotlight, and she was given the role of handling the press releases and managing social media for the hospital.

She signed on to her computer and checked her emails. She found nothing too urgent; just a few upcoming events to post on their Facebook and Twitter pages. She checked the local news, searching for any stories related to Orlando Memorial Medical Center, and then she went back to their Facebook page. The last post was five days old, so she posted some educational content from their website along with an upcoming event, a Health Fair the following week in their cafeteria, open to the public. She also posted a photo and a welcome to one of the new cardiologists they recently hired.

Then she clicked on Twitter. She knew she hadn't posted anything there since the previous Monday. She didn't get as much reaction from Twitter as she did from Facebook, so she didn't focus on it so much. Besides, the last thing she read indicated that only twenty percent of Twitter users were in the US.

When the @OrlMemMC page loaded, Terry was surprised to find thirty notifications. Normally there were only one or two. When she began reading them, an uncomfortable feeling caused her to sit upright and pay closer attention.

A Twitter user named @CriticalCoverUp had posted several tweets directed toward @OrlMemMC, and the news wasn't good. One tweet mentioned nurses being instructed to clock out for lunches they never actually took. Another suggested doctors were paid based on the number of procedures they perform, rather than on their level of expertise. They posts were full of hashtags regarding fraud and unfair labor practices. All of them included the hashtag #CriticalCoverUp.

There were a few more from the same Twitter user, but even more alarming were the retweets with comments by other users. She'd have to investigate who these users were, but a few were easily identifiable and much more worrisome. One was from @LeapfrogGroup, an important health care watchdog organization, and another from its partner, @HospSafetyGrade, which rates hospitals based on patient safety. Another was from a large, well-known law firm in Orlando.

Before Terry even finished perusing the tweets, which had all been posted within the past week, she texted her boss, Ed McManus, the director of public relations. She thought he was in a meeting but hoped he'd look at his texts. He did so and texted a reply, explaining that the meeting was wrapping up and he'd call her in ten minutes.

While she waited for Ed's call, she continued perusing the tweets. In the middle of reading them, another notification came in. This one was from the local news station, @WFTV. Terry shook her head and cringed as she read it: "What's going on in our hospitals? We're on this #WFTVInvestigates," followed by the original tweet by @CriticalCoverUp suggesting cardiologists were stashing beer in the cath lab and partying after procedures.

Realizing the renewed urgency of the situation, Terry texted Ed again. "Need you immediately. Can't wait. Crisis."

Two minutes later, Ed strolled into IT and headed for Terry's desk. "What was so urgent that it couldn't wait five more minutes?" he asked, obviously annoyed at having to cut his meeting short.

"Read this and you'll see." She turned her computer monitor around so he could see the screen.

As he read the tweets, he scowled and furrowed his brows. In a raised voice, he asked, "What is this about? When did this post?"

Pointing to the screen, Terry answered, "This one about the cath lab just posted from WFTV News. That's why I knew you needed to see it now, before the TV crews arrive."

"Jesus, Terry, this is a crisis! I'm sorry I didn't come immediately." Ed texted CEO Rob Chapman, Chief of Staff Dr. John Petry, and Katharine Jenkins, risk manager, to alert them of the emergency. "911 - PR crisis concerning cardiologists. TV news covering. Call me immediately for details so we know how to proceed when the media calls us."

News travels with lightning speed on Twitter, and Ed seemed grateful that the tweet from the TV station hadn't come in over the weekend and gone unnoticed. He reviewed the other tweets with Terry and began formulating a response for Twitter and a plan to deal with the media outlets to minimize any major fallout before the hospital could conduct their own investigation.

"Reply to that tweet, Terry, the one from @WFTV, and say something about Orlando Memorial Medical Center investigating unverified reports related to cardiologists drinking in the cath lab. Add something about ethics and compliance too. You know the best words to use."

She got right on it, posting the tweet as he suggested, hoping to minimize the damage that had already been done.

***

Ed had been back in his office less than two minutes when the hospital CEO called. "What's going on, Ed? Do we have a PR emergency?"

"Yes, Rob, we do, and time is of the essence." Ed explained about the tweets and asked for direction as to how to proceed. "We've already issued a reply to the tweet, but we need to at least say something when the media arrives. Without any verified information about this alleged cath lab incident, I can give a brief statement saying this is the first we've heard anything about the issue and talk about our commitment to our ethics program. We should say that we're going to be conducting an internal investigation. Or we can have the chief of staff give a similar statement and limit questions, whichever you prefer. I also texted Petry and Jenkins."

"Okay. I agree with your first suggestion. If Petry is available, I can get him to talk too. I think he may have surgery this morning though."

"And there's more," Ed said. He informed the CEO about the specific tweets mentioning their hospital. "I don't know who this @CriticalCoverUp is, but they've been posting all sorts of negative things about us, stuff having to do with patient safety, employee satisfaction, nursing shortages . . . the list goes on."

"This isn't good."

Ed's stomach churned and suddenly he had a pounding headache. This was not going to be a good week.

Chapter 48

Allison slept late and spent a leisurely morning sipping coffee, checking her emails, and giving Snowball some special attention. It was after noon by the time she signed onto the Twitter site. What she found pleased her immensely—one hundred notifications and fifty more followers. She scrolled through them, happy to see that major regulatory agencies like the American Health Quality Association, The Joint Commission, and Centers for Medicare and Medicaid Services were not only following her, but they'd replied and retweeted.

What amazed her most was that the local news had picked up her tweets and replied, followed by a response, for the first time, from the hospital. She could barely contain her excitement, knowing Critical Cover-Up had become an entity to be taken seriously. *The shit's going to hit the fan . . . if it hasn't already!* she thought as her fingers flew across the keyboard.

She quickly searched Google to see if any news stories had been posted yet and found one from the WFTV website under Breaking News: "Investigating reports of inappropriate physician behavior and more at Orlando

Memorial Medical Center." Allison read the short article, which mentioned the tweet about the cath lab and said the news organization was waiting to interview hospital personnel. A brief reply from the hospital indicated they were investigating the unverified report themselves.

Excited was not a strong enough term for the feeling she had. *Wired* might be more accurate. She didn't know if Paula was awake yet, but she texted her and Tracy anyway. "Have you seen the news? I think we're being taken seriously. Call me." She added a link to the news story.

Tracy texted back first. "Am at work. The place is going crazy. Can't talk now."

So the shit had *hit the fan!* Allison grinned. Sean would be thrilled if he knew what was happening.

Paula called Allison as soon as she read the text. "Just waking up. Fill me in."

Unable to contain her enthusiasm, Allison elaborated. "I couldn't wait to tell you what's happened. We made the news!"

"What do you mean?" a sleepy Paula asked.

Allison explained the whole story to Paula and told her that Tracy texted her, saying the hospital was going crazy.

"Oh wow. There's no going back now."

"You know it, Paula. This is just the start. And do you realize that JCAHO and other regulatory agencies are following us now? This is much more than I had hoped for, and it's only the beginning," an impassioned Allison said.

"I guess we'll be headed to Cali sooner rather than later then. I don't know when they'll discover who's behind Critical Cover-Up. In a way, I wouldn't mind if they did find out. I'm proud of what we're doing," Paula said.

"Yeah, it'll be good to be fully prepared before the time comes."

"Let's get to California first, and then they can find out anything they want."

"Okay. I need to get back to the Twitter account and start posting these news stories on the website too. The more who see it, the better the exposure. Our aim is to increase awareness and let the others do their investigating. I love being behind the scenes. See you tonight at work. By then the story should be on TV. I'm setting my DVR to record."

Twitter was busy and the notifications continued to roll in. Allison responded and retweeted, following accounts that had engaged with her and other accounts that seemed like good contacts. She also added the Twitter feed to the criticalcoverup.com website, hoping to draw more traffic from the website to Twitter.

Then she tweeted out some more replies and scheduled tweets for the next forty-eight hours:

> Hospital under investigation for ethics violations @OrlMemMC #criticalcoverup @CMSGov @ahahospitals @WESH

> Does your hospital violate patient safety goals? Tweet #CriticalCoverUp @CriticalCoverUp @TJCommission We can help.

And there were several more like this one:

> Unfair labor practices reported by physicians and nurses @OrlMemMC denied by hospital administration #CriticalCoverUp @NLRB @ahahospitals #Unfairlabor.

Allison realized that any vague tweet suggesting an impropriety could glean attention and possibly a retweet. Nothing could hurt, and, at best, the stories would be publicized and scrutinized.

She posted the news story from WFTV on the website and searched for others, but it was still too early. The evening news would be on when she was on her way to work, but she knew she'd hear plenty when she arrived.

***

When Paula drove onto the hospital grounds, she passed four news trucks set up for broadcasting. A crowd gathered on the hospital lawn, and people stood huddled in groups of three or four, heads together as if in serious conversation. *Oh boy, here we go.* She parked in the garage and headed inside, clocking in a few minutes early. Eager to learn what was going on, she put her bag away and went to the nurses' station to check out her assignment and get a feel for the latest developments. She didn't have to wait long. Tracy came right over to her and filled her in.

"It's been crazy all day. The news got wind of the story about the cardiologists drinking in the cath lab, and administration has been around all day. They've sent out emails warning us not to talk to the press. I think the TV crews are still out in front of the hospital."

"Yes, I saw them when I came in. I guess we've opened up Pandora's box, to use an old cliché," Paula said.

"Please reassure me that my name will be kept out of this. I can't afford to lose my job, you know. My husband would kill me if he knew I'd gotten involved."

Margie Miklas

"Don't worry, Tracy. Allison would never compromise you. She gave you her word, and I won't say anything either. This thing is snowballing though. Allison told me she's been posting on Twitter and the website, and tons of hospital watchdog groups and regulatory agencies have followed us. Also, as you can see, the news channels are on the story. We're hoping to get a major cable news network like CNN to engage with @CriticalCoverUp too."

"I'm anxious to see the evening news," Tracy said, "and what the hospital's response is. Anyway, I know you need to get report. I gave you a 1:1 assignment. You've had your share of triples lately."

"Thanks, Tracy," Paula said.

Paula got report and was happy to have a critical but stable patient for a change. Maybe she'd have a chance to collaborate more with Allison if her assignment wasn't too bad. She was glad Allison was working, but equally thankful this was her last shift for a few days.

***

"This is Keisha Thomas from WFTV News, reporting tonight from Orlando Memorial Medical Center, where allegations of inappropriate and unethical behavior by physicians have recently come to light via Twitter. The Twitter account, @CriticalCoverUp, posted this tweet, and we are now one of several news organizations trying to find out more details." The reporter went on to read the tweet about alleged cath lab parties, quoting each hashtag for her viewers.

"I have a spokesperson from the hospital here with me. This is Ed McManus, director of public relations for

Orlando Memorial Medical Center. Good evening, Ed. What can you tell us about these disturbing allegations?"

"Thank you, Keisha. I was just as surprised as you to learn of this today over social media, and while we are conducting our own internal investigation, I want to emphasize that these reports are completely and totally unverified. We are proud of our cath lab here, and our cardiologists rank as some of the best in Florida. Of course, we are committed to the highest standards of ethics and integrity at Orlando Memorial Medical Center, and if we do find any truth to these outrageous reports, any possible misconduct, then of course we will be transparent and deal with the situation in every conceivable way. I'd like to introduce Dr. John Petry, the chief of staff, for his perspective on the situation. Thank you." McManus stepped away as the cameraman focused on Dr. Petry.

"Good evening. While I have not yet had a chance to discuss these reports in detail with the cardiologists, I can tell you that I find them offensive and would be surprised if there is any basis to them. We will fully comply with hospital ethical standards and the law, if we discover the slightest impropriety. That's all for now. Thank you."

Keisha continued with her reporting. "Well, there you have it. The hospital is taking no questions at this time and denies any knowledge regarding the allegations of misconduct in the cath lab. WFTV is continuing its investigation into these allegations and is also working to track down the owner of the Twitter site, @CriticalCoverUp and its connected website, criticalcoverup.com. We will update you as soon as we have further information. Reporting tonight from Orlando Memorial Medical Center, I'm Keisha Thomas for WFTV News."

After briefing the news crew, the hospital administrators made rounds throughout the hospital to personally inform each department of the hospital's statement and warn them about any discussions with news outlets or on their personal social media accounts. It was obvious to the staff that this was a huge deal and the administration was worried.

When the hospital administrators showed up in SICU, Allison and Paula had already been working for an hour and were interested in hearing the message and observing the attitude of the VIPs. They put on a good show, but were definitely in defense mode. Allison and Paula listened and asked no questions, unlike some of their colleagues. They knew to fly under the radar, as this would be the best way to handle the situation.

After their shift, Paula waited for Allison, who had to give report on three patients. "Wait until they get wind of the other stuff we put out there. I don't even know if they know about it yet. Nothing was mentioned."

Allison agreed. "I doubt if they heard yet. They had to address this because it's egregious; plus, the news had it. There will be a lot more in the coming days. Even though I have to work the next two nights, before I got to bed I'll make time to check Twitter and post the news story that aired last night. I plan to get up early this afternoon so I can reply to our notifications and tweet stuff targeted directly to more news agencies. I'm pumped up, as you can see. You need to catch up on your rest after working all these nights in a row, I'll touch base later, okay?"

Paula nodded in agreement as they walked out of the hospital together. "Yeah, I'm beat. See you later, Allison."

For the next three to four weeks, the onslaught was nonstop, and news crews from the rest of the state were camped outside the hospital. CNN had picked up the story, as had some of the print media and online newspapers such as the *New York Times*, the *Sun-Sentinel*, the *Miami Herald*, and the *Tampa Tribune*.

The hospital was reeling in the aftermath of continued accusations and daily news stories on television, online, and in print. The public relations department had to add another person to their staff to help respond to Twitter and answer comments on news stories. They had attempted to determine who was behind Critical Cover-Up, to no avail. Twitter accounts can be created simply by registering with an email address, which is not made available to the public. With no idea who they were up against, all they could do was fight back and try to stem the bleeding.

Repercussions were already occurring, with talk of mass resignations on some of the nursing units. Most of the travel nurse agencies reported that they couldn't get any nurses interested in working at Orlando Memorial Medical Center due to all the negative publicity about poor working conditions and patient safety situations. And elective surgeries were down by large percentages. Patients were choosing other area hospitals for their procedures. Admissions were down, and they'd had to close some beds. These were all major causes for concern, but the key fear was about losing funding, which would force them to close.

Medicare had already issued the dreaded Notice of Immediate Jeopardy letter, an extremely serious adverse action. The letter stated that the hospital was not in compliance with one or more conditions of participation, and this caused, or could cause, serious injury, harm, impairment, or death to its patients. Orlando Memorial Medical Center was then required to take immediate steps to submit a plan of correction to remove this jeopardy. If the entire situation couldn't be resolved within twenty-three days, the hospital would lose its funding and be terminated from Medicare and/or Medicaid programs. The hospital would no longer be able to function under those conditions.

Chapter 49

Paula had been in San Jose for six weeks and was already in love with California. *I should have done this years ago. I feel so alive, and I'm not killing myself at the hospital.* Exactly as she had heard, the working conditions were great, and she never had more than two patients. She had a comfortable apartment and was doing more socially than she ever had in Orlando.

"You'd love it here, Allison," she said one day as the two chatted on the phone. "When does your travel assignment start? The hospital is great, a big change from Orlando."

"I bet, Paula. I'm so happy you like it out there. There was a delay with my California license, and I'm still waiting. I think it had to do with the transcripts getting forwarded from my school. They think it will only be another week or two."

"So how are things back there? Did you turn in your resignation? What about Tracy?"

"Yeah, I left last week. Everything's falling apart for the hospital, unfortunately, but they brought it on themselves. They somehow were able to maintain their

Medicare credentialing, but I think it's just a matter of time. They're trying to improve nurse-patient ratios, but it's not consistent. They don't have enough nurses, because people have quit, and no one wants to work there, despite a sign-on bonus.

"Tracy saw the writing on the wall and got hired at Florida Hospital in their CVICU. They're even going to train her to do open-hearts. She'll be a staff nurse. None of that middle-management responsibility. Her last day is tomorrow, I think."

"Cool. Good for her. Are you still spending a lot of time on the website and Twitter accounts?"

"Yes, I am, Paula. It's good I'm not working, actually, because this is taking up almost all my time. So many other facilities have the same issues, and we're exposing them on social media, making people aware. Part of me wants to go public with this, you know, give lectures, go on talk shows, maybe even write a book. I don't know. *Hell, maybe even apply to law school.* I feel like I'm really making a difference with Critical Cover-Up."

"I'm getting some weird vibes here. Are you sure you're still planning to come to California?"

"Oh, I'm going to come. Trust me. It's just that I believe in this project and think I could make a full-time business out of it. Hire lawyers and really accomplish some things."

"But don't you need to work as a nurse to have enough income to live on until the business is doing well enough to make a profit?"

"Sure. I'm not independently wealthy. I was thinking about coming out there to do a travel assignment and then coming back here. Maybe do thirteen weeks and take three months off. I'd make enough in those thirteen weeks to be able to cruise the next thirteen. Besides, I didn't tell you, but Sean named me as a beneficiary on his life insurance policy."

"Really? No, you never told me."

"Well, I felt kind of weird about it. But the more I think about it, he'd be smiling knowing what I was doing. If that money could help in any way, it would make him happy. I know it. So, part of me is doing this with Sean at my side."

"You really loved him, didn't you?"

"I did. I didn't realize how much until he was gone though. You don't get a second chance too often in life, so I don't want to screw this up. Although the original idea of Critical Cover-Up was mine, you and Tracy helped make it a reality. I believe in my heart that we were able to change some things. But I see a bigger picture and think I can change a whole lot more.

You know, Paula, I never told you this, but I almost died in a bad car accident when I was in my twenties, long before I became a nurse. It made me realize that life is short, and I want to take advantage of every opportunity while it's there. It may be gone tomorrow."

"I hear you, Allison, and I'm good with that. I do hope you come out here, but I'm a big girl and can manage here alone too. Who knows, with the social scene out here, maybe I'll find someone special."

"You're right, Paula. Who knows?"

About the Author

An award-winning author, Margie Miklas is a recently retired critical care nurse, social media manager, and travel blogger. As a career critical care nurse with a specialty in cardiovascular nursing, Margie has experienced a wide range of changes in the world of healthcare. When she's not writing, she enjoys traveling to Italy, spending time with her family, and relaxing at the beach. She makes her home in Florida and is a member of the Florida Writers Association.

Follow Margie on Facebook
https://www.facebook.com/MargieMiklasAuthor

Follow Margie on Twitter https://twitter.com/MargieMiklas

Follow Margie on Instagram www.instagram.com/margiemiklas/

Follow her blog, *Margie in Italy* https://margieinitaly.com